Death
of a Postman

Death
of a Postman

John Creasey

PERENNIAL LIBRARY

Harper & Row, Publishers, New York
Cambridge, Philadelphia, San Francisco, Washington
London, Mexico City, São Paulo, Singapore, Sydney

This book was originally published in England under the title *Parcels For Inspector West*. A hardcover edition of *Death of a Postman* was published in the United States in 1956 by Harper & Brothers.

First PERENNIAL LIBRARY edition published 1987.

Library of Congress Cataloging-in-Publication Data
Creasey, John.
  Death of a postman.
  I. Title.
PR6005.R517D4   1987   823'.912   87-45035
ISBN 0-06-080890-X (pbk.)

87 88 89 90 91 OPM 10 9 8 7 6 5 4 3 2 1

Death
of a Postman

1

The Party

The police car turned the corner of the ill-lit suburban street. Lamps, standing at regular intervals, were misty yellow. Few windows showed lights, but here and there a number glowed yellow against a pale glass fanlight, and Sergeant Kilby, sitting next to Chief Inspector Roger West, called out these numbers in a monotonous voice.

"Twenty-eight," he said.

West made no comment, but switched on the headlights. The beams showed up a couple in a doorway, arms round each other, the youth turning a ghostlike face toward the car. His right hand was on the girl's head, pressing it against his shoulder, as if he was making quite sure that no one could see who she was.

Kilby grinned.

"That'll teach 'em! Forty-two."

West was still silent. The couple passed behind them and a man holding a small white dog on a leash appeared from a doorway and turned in the other direction. They soon passed him. West put

1

the car into neutral and then switched off the engine and they glided with hardly a sound, gloom all about them except where the headlights shone.

"Sixty," said Kilby. "Nearly there." He gave West a quick, rather surprised glance, as if at last he began to wonder why West was silent to a point of surliness. "Nasty job for you, sir."

"Yes," said West.

"Sixty-eight—next door but one," said Kilby. "It's the one with the lights on in the front room. Got *their* decorations up early, haven't they?"

"Looks like it," said West, and the car stopped immediately outside the front door of Number 72 Clapp Street, Fulham—the London surburb adjoining Chelsea, where he lived. "No, sit here for a minute." He took out a cigarette case and proffered it, to Kilby's surprise. Kilby hadn't worked with Roger West before, and knew him only by his reputation; he was beginning to believe that part of it was unjustified, for West was supposed to be a good man to work with.

West flicked a lighter. Kilby pushed the end of his cigarette into it.

"Thank you, sir."

The sound of piano music came from the window of Number 72 Clapp Street, a gaiety which contrasted sharply with West's manner, just then. The lilting song "Do ye ken John Peel with his coat so gray."...Children seemed to be singing as much as grownups. More. It wasn't possible to be sure, because net curtains were drawn halfway across the window, and in the middle of the window was a Christmas tree. The tree was tall and wide and decked with colored lights and tinsel, with hanging frost and crackers, topped with a fairy and her wand, all showing as clearly as it could from outside. The light inside the room looked bright, and shadowy figures kept moving.

The singing and the music stopped.

"Not exactly Christmassy news," Kilby said. He felt awkward, partly because of West's manner, partly because West had made him feel a heel. He remembered, now, that West also had a reputation for being "soft"; he could be as tough as they came, but sometimes took other people's troubles too hard. That wasn't good in a copper, and it wasn't one of Kilby's faults, but here was the sergeant smoking West's cigarette and watching the party and feeling sheepish. He felt that he had to say something to defend himself.

"There's one thing," he said, "half the married couples I know wouldn't really care if the other one died. Some would be cut up, I know, but most of them put up an act for a few weeks, and then start looking round for Number Two. Comes hard sometimes, though."

West took his cigarette from his lips.

"Yes," he said. "Bryant had five children."

"*Five* kids?"

"That's right," said West. "All in there. The second-eldest boy is nearly nineteen, and home for his seven days before going overseas. That's why they're having the Christmas party early. They'll be expecting their father any time now."

Kilby said, "How'd you know all this?"

"Bryant was going to have a couple of hours off, but several of his mates went down with flu, and with the Christmas rush beginning to build up, he worked on. I had a word with a friend of his at the

3

Sorting Office. Not much the matter with his married life, I gather."

Silence fell.

Then the piano started up again, and a child began to sing. The sound came clearly because the window was open a little at the top. A clear, sweet treble. *I'm dreaming of a white Christmas, da-da-di-da-di-da-di-da.* Now and again the singer faltered on the word. West sat still, the cigarette half finished, until the singing and the piano music stopped; there was a quick burst of applause, mostly handclapping.

A figure appeared at the window.

The net curtain was pushed aside and a woman's face showed for a moment, a woman with fair, curly hair. She was holding the curtain on one side. The glow of one of the red lamps of the Christmas-tree decoration made one cheek a pale red, and gave her a kind of vitality. Her eyes shone. She was obviously staring at the car and wondering why it was there; as obviously, she hadn't come to the window to look for it.

West said: "I'll get it over. You wait outside until I call for you, will you?"

"Yes, sir," Kilby said.

The curtain fell into place, and the woman disappeared. West got out of the car and rounded it, as Kilby stepped out on the other side. The street lamp showed West's face, set and almost somber.

"Damned good looker," Kilby thought, as West passed him. "Hates this like poison, but he didn't *have* to do it himself." Uneasily, Kilby watched as West went up to the front door and knocked. The sharp sound echoed up and down the street, crisp on the misty, frosty night. Singing started again; a

4

chorus. The colored lights sparkled on the tinsel and the hanging frost. West stood back a pace, as if prepared to wait for some time, but he didn't have to; the door opened at once, and the woman stood there.

The light of the narrow hall was behind her, and the light of the street lamp was on her face. What gave some people starry eyes? Kilby watched with the admiration he would feel for any pretty woman, until West moved again and his head hid her from Kilby's sight.

"Why the hell did it have to happen on *party* night?" Kilby muttered to himself.

He heard West speak, the woman answer; he saw her stand aside and West, carrying his hat, step into the small hall. The door closed. The singing seemed louder than ever and the piano was being thumped by someone with a much heavier hand than the first pianist, which was a pity. *While shepherds watched their flocks by night all seated on the ground, the angel of the Lord came down and glory shone around....Glad tidings of great joy I bring....*

"Oh, Gawd," breathed Kilby.

Roger West looked into Mrs. Bryant's blue eyes, into a puzzled, rather eager face; a piquant face. He knew that she was in her forties; she looked younger, although she didn't really look young. He had seen enought at the window to know that she had quite a figure for the mother of five, but he didn't see her figure now, just those shiny blue eyes—happy in spite of her surprise at having a visitor. She had a good, clear complexion, with

5

very little make-up and a dark dress caught high at the neck; he noticed the sleeves.

"Good evening," he said. "Are you Mrs. Bryant?"

"Yes," she said.

"I wonder if you could spare me a few minutes," West said, and that puzzled her still more.

He smiled.

It wasn't easy to summon up that smile. He could imagine the kind of blow that he was going to give this woman, and in one way he hated himself for it. He could have arranged for a dozen people to come and tell her that her husband was dead, but no, here he was. He'd known in advance about the party and that hadn't made it any easier. Bitterly he found himself wondering why someone had leaped out of the darkness and struck this woman's husband a murderous blow on the back of the head.

"Yes, of course," Mrs. Bryant said, "come in."

He stepped past her, and she closed the front door, shutting Kilby off. West paused. Mrs. Bryant hurried past the door of the front room, which was ajar. A small boy, about seven or eight, put a head round the door as if anxious to find out what was detaining his mother. "Stay there," Mrs. Bryant ordered, and there was a slightly different note in her voice, as if something of the truth had dawned on her; or fear of some kind had touched her.

"You won't mind coming into the kitchen, will you?" she asked. "It's all ready for the party tea. We're waiting until my husband comes home."

West didn't speak.

She opened the kitchen door. It was a long room, with a narrow table in the middle—two long boards on trestles placed together and covered with white tablecloths. Out here, the colorfulness of the Christmas tree was put in the shade. Here was a party table spread to delight every eye; at each place a jelly, red, green, orange or yellow; at each place, two crackers; and everywhere, jam tarts and mince tarts, bowls of fruit, iced cakes and plain cakes. In the middle of all of this, as if lording it over the rest, was a huge Christmas cake, beautifully decorated with Santa Clause and his reindeer sleigh heading for a house set in the snow. Paper chains festooned the ceiling and the wall, and over this doorway and the doorway leading to a scullery beyond was a sprig or two of mistletoe.

"What is it you want?" asked Mrs. Bryant.

There was no way of breaking news of this kind gently; hardly any way in which West could prepare her.

He wondered how she would react.

He also wondered who else was in the front room; sister or brother or someone other than the children to whom Mrs. Bryant could turn for help.

If she hadn't looked so fresh, so eager and vivacious, it would have been easier.

She raised her hand. "Please—"

"Mrs. Bryrant," West said, "I only wish I hadn't to bring you such bad news, but I have."

She caught her breath, and the brightness faded out of her eyes. The silence, which West had almost dreaded, lasted for a long time; it was made worse by another burst of singing from the front room.

Good King Wenceslas looked out . . .

"Tom," Mrs. Bryant breathed, and her eyes cried: "No!"

"I'm desperately sorry," West said. "Yes. I'm a police officer, Mrs. Bryant, and it's my job to try to find out just why it happened and who did it." He paused, to let her understand just what he meant and when he saw her put both hands in front of her breast, and saw the color draining from her cheeks, leaving them so pale, her lips so red and her eyes so brilliant a blue, he moved a little closer, because she might faint, and he didn't want her to fall.

He said quietly: "If I do or say anything that is in any way hurtful, it is simply because I'm trying to do my job. And if there's anything at all I can do to help, please tell me."

Now, she stood quite still, until he believed that the risk of her fainting had passed.

"What—what happened?"

"All we know is that he was attacked near the Post Office, on his way home," West said. "He died very quickly."

Bryant's wife didn't cry out. She didn't move her arms. The color was still draining from her cheeks, and it seemed to Roger West that life itself was draining out of her; that a kind of death was replacing it. In those few seconds, she grew visibly older.

The first Noel, the angels did say...

Mrs. Bryant stared into West's face, without looking away, as if she derived some kind of strength from him. He didn't know how, but at times he seemed to be able to help others simply by being at hand; as if the sufferer, now Bryant's widow, sensed that in some odd way he felt almost the same horror as she.

Then she spoke in a low-pitched, empty voice.

"Will you—will you please go to the front room and—and ask my—my son's fiancée to come here

8

for a minute? Her name is—is May. And make sure that none of the children follow her. Will you—will you be so good?"

"I'll fetch her," Roger West promised, and turned to go along the narrow passage. The carol was being sung as heartily as a carol could be. He took three long strides, and then Mrs. Bryant called sharply:

"Please!"

He turned round quickly.

"We mustn't spoil anything for the children," she breathed, "we mustn't—"

And then she began to cry.

2

The Fiancée

A girl in a red party frock and pigtails, aged ten or eleven, came to the door first, eyes bright with curiosity. Roger asked for May. "May!" cried this girl, without moving. "May!" In a moment a young woman of about twenty appeared. She had dark hair, attractive freshness and pleasant features. As she reached the door, she was smiling. Then she sensed seriousness, and spoke to the younger girl. "You go and join the others," she said, and stepped into the passage and pulled the door to.

"I'm May," she declared. "Did you want to speak to me?"

"I had to bring Mrs. Bryant some bad news," Roger said, "and she asked me to fetch you."

"*Bad* news! Not about—" May began. She caught her breath, but soon went on with a rush: "Dad's all right, isn't he?" So she was really one of the family.

"No," said Roger, and added deliberately: "Mr. Bryant was murdered this afternoon."

It probably sounded brutal, but he believed that

it was the right way to tell this girl. Quality had a way of showing itself, and here was quality.

Silence...

She said, in a funny little voice: "Oh, poor Mother," and turned swiftly and went hurrying along to the kitchen. Roger followed more slowly. Mrs. Bryant was sitting on a chair near the table, with her head buried in her hands and her shoulders shaking. Her movements made the jellies on the table shake; a riot of dancing color mocking at tragedy. Spoons, knives and forks jingled. A silly song came into Roger's mind and he couldn't force it out. *Jingle bells, jingle bells, jingle all the day.* Day or way? May went to Bryant's wife, put her hands on her shoulders and stood with her back to Roger. She wore a pale blue dress, fitting close to her waist, and the curve of her hips was lovely. Her legs were beautiful. She didn't speak or move, but gradually the older woman's crying quieted. Roger stood in the hall, listening to the singing and then to talking; children's voices predominated. He wondered whether the party would go on, whether either of these women would have the moral strength to see it through; then he found himself wondering whether they should.

Mrs. Bryant moved.

"All right—May," she said. It was a croak of a voice, and made Roger turn quickly. "May," she went on, "tell Micky and the others that—that I've had to go out. Don't tell them why, just say—say Mrs. Emery's ill again or something like that. See they get their tea. Don't—don't spoil it for them, May, *please.*"

"I'll see to it," May promised, in a low voice. "But—what will you do?" When Mrs. Bryant

11

didn't answer at once, she burst out: "What a wicked thing to happen! What a swine of a man!"

"May, *don't*."

"We'll find out who it was, soon," Roger West put in, sliding smoothly back into the conversation. "Do you intend to go to friends, Mrs. Bryant?"

"Yes, just across—just across the road."

"I'll see you there. Are there any other adults in the front room?"

"Oh, yes," said May. "Don't worry about us, we'll be all right. Mum, are you sure—"

"They've been looking forward to this party for *weeks*," Mrs. Bryant began. "I can't—"

She couldn't finish.

Ten minutes later, Mrs. Bryant was out in the street with Roger West. She had slipped on a heavy blue coat, but no hat. It wasn't really cold, but more misty than it had been; if this kept up for long the night would soon be really foggy. The haloes round the street lamps were less sharply defined. Kilby was coming toward them, but didn't speak when he saw Roger walking across the road with the woman. The house they went to appeared to be in darkness.

Before Roger knocked, Mrs. Bryant said: "I want—I want to know exactly what happened, please."

"Let's see if your friend is in," Roger said. "I'll tell you more then."

He knocked.

"Please," said Mrs. Bryant, "I would like to know."

And she meant to.

"It's very simple," Roger said. "Your husband was taking the short cut from River Way to the Embankment, and was struck from behind. The doctors are quite certain that he didn't know what had happened. He had no warning, and it was over very quickly." Roger still hoped that, even in the grief of this moment, assurance would help.

Mrs. Bryant asked: "Are you sure about that?"

"Absolutely sure."

"I see," she said. She stared at the dark door, and Roger knocked again. "It looks as if Rosa's out," she said to herself. "If she doesn't answer soon I'd better go to Mrs. Featherstone's." They stood close together outside the little door. "When —when did it happen?"

"A little after five o'clock."

"He—he promised to leave by five at the latest."

"So I was told."

"But *why* should it happen to Tom?" she cried.

"We're finding out," Roger said. "Scotland Yard is doing everything it can. The men at the River Way Sorting Office are being questioned too, and we're searching for anyone who was near the alley. But I needn't go into detail, Mrs. Bryant, just be sure that everything possible is being done to find the murderer."

Silence.

Then:

"Murdered," she said, in an agonized voice. "My Tom, murdered. Oh, God, why should it happen to him?" She fell silent again, but had turned to face Roger; suddenly she gripped his arms, and the strength in her fingers was so great that it hurt. "Why should it happen to Tom? He was so good, everyone liked him, everyone. A better man never

13

lived." She shook Roger, fiercely. "I mean that, I'm not just saying it because he's dead, a better man never lived! He was so kind to everyone, he loved —*he loved life*." Now, she gripped Roger's arms so tightly that it was really painful. She seemed to be fighting down the sob in her voice. "Oh, God, how shall I tell Micky? How shall I tell the younger children? To be struck down like that, to be alive one moment and dead the next, it—it's so *awful*."

"Yes," Roger said, and knocked at the door again, but that was only a gesture; there was little hope that her friend would be in. "Hadn't we better go to Mrs. Featherstone's?"

"I suppose we had," consented Mrs. Bryant, but suddenly there was no feeling in her voice. Just emptiness. "I wish Rosa was in, she—she would understand so much more, she—"

She broke off.

Someone was walking briskly along the street, on the other side; a man and woman. He wondered if this could be the Rosa whom Mrs. Bryant was talking about, but the couple passed, and were hidden for a moment by Roger's car.

"Mr.—" Mrs. Bryant began, and then gave a choky little laugh, the kind of sound which suggested that hysteria wasn't far away. "I don't even know who you are," she said, "only that you're a policeman."

"My name is West—Chief Inspector West." Roger took out a card and proffered it, but she didn't even glance at it. "Which way is Mrs. Featherstone's?"

"I don't think I'll go there, after all," said Mrs. Bryant, "I don't think it would really help. She'd be very kind, but she would talk so much and—"

she broke off again. "I'm sorry to behave like this, I hardly know what I'm saying, but they *must* finish the party. *They must finish the party!* All that work, all that trouble, all that longing for it, I couldn't stand it if they were told before the party was over. Please," she went on, pathetically, "let them enjoy the party."

Now, he was holding her right arm.

"Come on." he said briskly. "My home is only ten minutes' drive from here; we'll go there. My wife will be in." He knew that his wife would drop everything and do anything to help. "It's no trouble at all," he said, above Mrs. Bryant's protests, and he guided her across the road. Kilby, sensing that he was wanted, came along smartly; the street lights showed the bewilderment in his expression. "Sergeant," Roger said, "I'm taking Mrs. Bryant to some friends. I want you stay here until I get back, or send someone to relieve you. Don't say anything to anyone."

"Right, sir."

Roger had opened the door of the seat next to the driving wheel. Mrs. Bryant got in, as if in a dream. Roger slid into his seat beside her, but before he closed the door a new light appeared at the end of the street; the dipped head lamp of a motorcycle. He heard the sharp beat of the engine, and then Mrs. Bryant exclaimed:

"Wait, please!" She wound down her window swiftly and looked out. Roger could just hear her voice. "It might be Derek, it might—it *is* Derek! *Derek!*" Now, she was almost beside herself, and Roger didn't try to restrain her but got out and hurried round to the other side of the car as the motorcyclist drew up.

The engine stopped on Mrs. Bryant's shout. "...ek!" was a screech.

"Hey, what's all this?" The man on the motorcycle was young and dark-helmeted. "Mum, what—"

"Derek, something terrible's happened to your father," Mrs. Bryant said quiveringly, "May's looking after the children; they *must* finish the party. You go in and help; she'll feel much better now you're here, but don't breathe a word to anyone else, don't spoil anything for them."

"Of course I won't," said Derek Bryant, with the overconfidence of self-assured youth. "But I don't get it. What's this something terrible that's happened to Dad?"

There was a pause; agonizing.

Then: "He's—*dead.*"

Derek seemed to sway backward. "*No*".

"I'm an officer from New Scotland Yard," Roger broke in, "and Sergeant Kilby here will tell you anything else you wish to know. I'm taking your mother to my home until the party is over." Unless this talking stopped, a crowd would collect. "Sergeant Kilby, give Mr. Bryant any help and information he needs."

"Yes, sir."

"But, Mum!" "All that cocky assurance melted in that cry. "Mum!"

"Go—go and help May," his mother said.

After another tense moment, Derek Bryant turned away.

Soon, Roger and Mrs. Bryant were back in the car.

Roger started the engine and eased off the clutch. He didn't go far, but pulled up round the corner of Clapp Street, took a flask from his hip pocket, unscrewed it, and said:

"Take a sip of this, Mrs. Bryant."

She did as he told her, and coughed; the smell of brandy came strongly. West took the flask back and slipped it into his pocket, then drove toward the Wandsworth Bridge Road, where he would turn left for Kings' Road and Chelsea. He hadn't stopped to ask himself why he was taking this woman to his own home; he didn't stop to ask himself what others would say about it. He simply knew that she needed much more help than most.

Mrs. Bryant leaned back, without speaking.

In less than ten minutes, Roger had pulled up outside his house in Bell Street. In another two, Mrs. Bryant was in the warm kitchen, where Janet West had blue paper packets of currants and sultanas, sugar and raisins, spread out on one end of the large table. A big mixing bowl contained a little flour and some candied peel. Janet, about the same height as Mrs. Bryant, was dark, with curly hair and gray-green eyes. She had a surprised and almost harassed look, as if bewildered by the interruption.

In a few sentences, she knew everything it was necessary to know, and quite suddenly and explosively, she said: "I'd like to hang some men myself!"

Mrs. Bryant, standing at a corner of the table and looking almost dazedly about her, glanced up and said unsteadily: "I—I know how you feel, but Tom—" she stopped, and screwed up her eyes; a moment later she went on in a high-pitched voice: "But my husband didn't believe in capital punishment. He always said that a murderer was men-

17

tally sick, no one would *kill* if he was normal. He—"

She dropped into a chair.

"Jan, I know you'll do everything you can," Roger said. "Mrs. Bryant was anxious not to break up a children's party. They're having it early because one of her sons is due to embark for overseas tomorrow. We'll get him compassionate leave, of course; tell her that."

Janet nodded, briskly.

"Where are the boys?" Roger asked.

"They're still at the gymnasium; its boxing finals night."

"Oh, yes," Roger said, "of course, I'll be back as soon as I can make it, and if I can't come myself I'll have a man with a car here in an hour or so. He can take Mrs. Bryant back when she's ready to go. All right?"

"You'd better get on," Janet said. She followed him to the door. "Have you caught anyone?"

"No."

"Well, catch this brute," Janet whispered in his ear, and then turned and hurried to Mrs. Bryant, ignoring the laden table and all the ingredients for the Christmas puddings. Roger didn't go for a moment, but watched. On the mantelpiece above the modern-type fireplace, with the boiler behind it, was a notice in flaming red, drawn by Martin, his elder son. It said:

9 SHOPPING DAYS TO CHRISTMAS

and beneath it Richard, the younger boy, had written:

HURRY UP!

18

It was good for a grin.

There wasn't anything else to grin about. Nine shopping days to Christmas, and a killer to find, hell burning already for Mrs. Bryant and hotting up for her children, and somewhere the murderer.

Roger was going out of the room when Mrs. Bryant cried: "*Stop!*"

He swung round, and she came rushing toward him. "I can't stay here," she cried. "I must see Tom. Do you understand, I must see my husband. Take me to him."

This sudden urge wasn't surprising; and if she saw her husband it might help her to the courage that she needed. Certainly there was no time to argue; she must have a quick yes or no.

"All right, Mrs. Bryant," Roger said. "I'll take you."

"I'll come, too," Janet decided briskly. "I'll just pop upstairs and get my coat."

She hurried off, leaving Roger and Mrs. Bryant together, and suddenly the woman began to talk more quickly and more freely. There was one question above all others that Roger wanted to ask her, and now she gave him the opportunity.

"How much money would your husband be likely to have with him, Mrs. Bryant?" He tried to sound casual.

"Oh, very little," Mrs. Bryant told him confidently. "Never more than a pound or two—*money* couldn't be the reason for it."

Roger didn't tell her, then, that the police had found a hundred pounds in the pocket of her husband's jacket.

3

Hotting Up

No one would ever have called Tom Bryant handsome. In death, he looked exactly what his wife had said that he was in life: a good man. This showed in the placid expression, the serenity, the hooked nose, the full lips. His thick, wavy hair was quite gray, suggesting that he was probably ten years older than this wife. Lying on the stone slab, he looked as much alive as dead, and his was the only body in the morgue.

Roger was on one side of Bryant's widow, Janet on the other.

They were not there long.

Without a word, Mrs. Bryant bent down, put her lips against a forehead which was already cold, then moved blindly toward the door. It was chilly in here, but warm outside in the passages. The warmth seemed to melt something inside her and she began to cry again, more freely than she had at home.

Roger and Janet went out with her into the Cannon Police Station adjoining, and Roger said:

"I'll have someone standing by to take you both home, Jan. If she wants to go back to Clapp Street, I'd let her."

"All right," said Janet. "Where are you going?"

"I'm going over to River Way, to see if our chaps have picked up anything," Roger said.

He didn't think that Mrs. Bryant noticed him leave.

Now that the harrowing part of the task was over he felt better; he could free himself from the harsh bite of another's grief, and see this as a job: to find a killer. He drove, alone, to River Way, which led to the Chelsea Embankment and the broad Thames. The huge new building of West London's Post Office stood as massive and in its way as commanding as the Battersea Power Station, only a mile or so away on the other side of the river. Every light at a thousand windows seemed to shine brightly. People could be seen sitting at desks near the windows. The great yard, approached by road from the Embankment, was crowded with jostling red post-office vans; traffic was on the move all the time. The new building dwarfed all others nearby, and in the misty gloom stood out like a monster with a thousand square eyes. Nonsense. Roger drove past it, seeing a police car at one gateway, and then slowed down toward the end of Goose Lane.

In Goose Lane, Bryant had been murdered.

It led from a side of the mammoth building to the Embankment, along which Bryant would have cycled home. It always saved him half a mile and a lot of traffic, and according to the Chief Sorter, whom Roger had seen earlier, many clerks and Sorting Office workers who lived in the southwest of London used that short cut—unless they traveled to and from work by bus, when it wouldn't help them. At the beginning and the end of the different shifts, it was used a great deal; between those rush hours, hardly at all. Normally, a single electric light shone at the near end of the lane; now, it was one of a dozen. Car headlights and a specially rigged searchlight were in position, so that the lane, which was usually very dark, was brighter than any floodlit stage. The bricks of the walls on either side showed up, and all their tiny holes looked black. It was even possible to see where the cement in between had started to crumble. At intervals there were alcoves, for the wall on one side had once been that of a private garden. The path was paved, but some of the old flagstones were cracked, and in places soil had gathered, especially at the sides and spots where the flagstones were broken.

At the far end was another wall lamp, helping to show that the lane was alive with men. There were the photographers, an inspector from Fingerprints with two sergeants, and other men taking measurements; all these had started before Roger had left, and should be well on with their job.

If they weren't, there would be trouble.

Roger turned into the alley and walked toward the men near the spot where Bryant had been found by another Post Office worker. This man could not have been three minutes behind Bryant; three minutes between life and death.

A crowd had gathered at the Embankment end, and uniformed policemen were keeping them back. The press was here in strength. One dead man, a dozen C.I.D. men, as many reporters hungry for news, a hundred sightseers—harbingers of thousands who would come next day.

Divisional as well as Yard men were here, and the Divisional Superintendent, Gorme, was officially in charge. Gorme was a big man, good in his steady way, who never lost a moment sending for Scotland Yard, preferring to make sure that he could at least share the responsibility, if anything went wrong.

"Hallo, Handsome," he greeted, "back already?" He sniffed. "Told the family?"

"Yes."

"Rather you than me, but I did offer."

''I know. Found anything?"

"We have and again we haven't," said Gorme, and gave another sniff; until one was used to that habit of his, it was annoying. "Footprints in the dirt at the side of the lane, made by a chap running. Well, might have been running—toe deep in some mud, heel hardly showing any impression at all. Bit of blood showing on the first three or four prints."

"Sent the blood for grouping?"

"Yes. If you ask me, chap might have killed Bryant and then run off on tiptoe to lessen sound. We took a cast after taking up the bloodstained bits."

"Nice work," said Roger. "Anything else?"

"Only the usual," Gorme said. "Got the area cordoned off while we search for more prints and a weapon. Know what I think?"

"He'd throw the weapon into the river."

Gorme grinned. "Two minds with but a single," he chanted. "Thought I'd wait for you before calling in the River boys. Like me to, now?"

"Will you?" asked Roger.

"Like a shot, Handsome, like a shot. Be seeing you." Gorme moved off, sniffing. Roger stood by himself for a few minutes, and no one in the lane took any particular notice of him. Most of the men were gathered round a spot where there were a lot of chalk marks on the ground, made when a man from the Yard had drawn a line to show the position of the body. The men taking measurements from this, so as to establish the exact position of the body, were finishing their job; so were the photographers. One man stood close to the wall, while another shone a powerful torch; he was scraping something off the weather-worn brickwork.

Roger neared him.

"What have you got there?"

"Blood spots," the man with the torch said flatly. "Highest is at seven feet two inches."

"Upward splash, eh?"

"Not much doubt about it, sir. We're just scraping off enough to make sure it's new blood, and to check the group."

"Right," said Roger.

He felt something soft beneath his feet, and looked down. Sawdust was spread thick, and it would be spread thickest over blood. This was close to one of the alcoves, where the murderer had lurked. Why should a man lurk here to strike down a Post Office sorter?

The medical evidence suggested that only two blows had been struck, one on top of the head, one a little lower down; perhaps as Bryant had been falling. Two blows—and the skull had cracked and broken. Smack, smack. Someone with exceptional strength—

Hold it.

Bryant's skull might have been thinner than the average. When they had the facts they would start working with them.

Roger went further along the lane and saw other spots chalked off, with a policeman on guard. Sightseers were only about thirty yards away. Inside one chalked circle was a pale blotch—this was the spot where the cast of a footprint had been taken. Roger went down on one knee and shone his torch onto it. A narrow toe mark showed, but there was hardly any impression of the heel. Gorme was always literal.

The routine work would be done as well without as with him, Roger knew, and he went back to his car. Gorme was coming away from his, wiping his lips with the back of his hand; he had a reputation for liking his liquor, but that didn't affect his sniff.

"The River boys will be on the job right away," he said. "We should have the doctor's report soon, and find out a bit about the weapon."

Roger said dryly: "Blunt instrument."

Gorme grinned.

Roger slid into his own car, flicked on the radio and talked to Scotland Yard. The footprint cast was already there, photographs were being developed and more casts were being made from the original. The medical report was confirmed by X-ray photographs—only two blows had been delivered. No one suggested that Bryant's skull had been particularly thin.

Roger could almost hear Mrs. Bryant's voice.

"Why *Tom?*"

Yes—why a Post Office sorter?

And why did a Post Office sorter earning less than ten pounds a week have a hundred pounds in his pocket?

Roger drove into the big yard of the River Way building. There were fewer red vans. Half a dozen big lorries carrying printed labels reading *Royal Mail* were the forerunners of the countless private lorries and vans which would soon be hired. The loading platform was piled high with parcels which had been brought from the nearby offices and were being tossed into different chutes—each big city had one of its own, like Birmingham, Manchester, Bristol, Cardiff, Edinburgh; there werc dozens. Other chutes were marked East Midlands, Southeast England, Home Counties, Western Isles, Ireland and the like. Men in dark blue stood by the mass of parcels which came off the vans and fed the chutes, and the parcels were swallowed up. Somewhere out of sight the same kind of thing was happening with letters. The new River Way Post Office was the largest in London, and was hotting up for the Christmas rush.

Roger was recognized by a one-armed lift attendant who took him up to the third floor and the Postmaster's offices.

"Know your way all right, sir?"

"Yes, thanks."

"Terrible business, sir, and Tom Bryant especially."

Roger paused. "Why especially?"

"Well, if you'd known Tom you wouldn't have asked," the liftman said. "They don't come any better."

"Man without enemies, eh?"

"I should have thought so, sir."

"Don't know anyone who didn't share your opinion, do you?"

"To tell you the truth, sir," the liftman said, "I don't know a soul who didn't like Tom Bryant."

Roger said, "We'll get the brute," and went on. He tapped at a door marked *Postmaster* and it was opened at once by a middle-aged woman in a black skirt and a light gray sweater, with dark hair done in a bun at the back. She had a pleasant smile.

"I thought it might be you, sir. They're all together in the Postmaster's room."

"Thanks," said Roger.

The secretary opened the door, and he stepped into a spacious room. There were three men inside —the Postmaster himself, Matthew Farnley, short and stocky, with close-cut gray hair and a pronounced double chin; the Chief Sorter, a small man named Carmichael, and a big man who dwarfed both the others—Detective Inspector Turnbull of the C.I.D. Turnbull had the look of a lion and the body of one, too; a massive and powerful man, who could upset a lot of people. Apparently he had been on his best behavior, for neither Farnley nor Carmichael looked upset.

"Hallo, sir," Turnbull greeted; the "sir" was for effect, and was not even slightly obsequious. "Mr. Farnley has been very helpful, but I can't say we've got anywhere yet."

Farnley waved a square hand.

"Sit down, Mr. West, please. Cigarette?" He lit Roger's cigarette, then Turnbull's, then his own; Carmichael didn't smoke. Carmichael was a small man whom it would be easy to overlook in a crowd. His coat was a little too large for him. His forehead was lined and the skin around his eyes wrinkled, and he had pale, gingery hair which needed cutting.

"I only wish we could help you to clear up this shocking business quickly," the Postmaster said. "Shocking! And just when things are hotting up for the Christmas rush. Don't misunderstand me, Mr. West, I'm desperately sorry about Bryant, but the work *must* go on."

"No reason why we should stop it," Roger said dryly. "So Bryant had no known enemies in the building."

"Absolutely none," Farnley assured him. "None at all. Eh, Carmichael?"

Carmichael was a mumbler.

"None at all," Roger made out. "One of the most popular men, well-respected and well-liked." The last words were hardly audible, and the Chief Sorter fidgeted with his hands and feet. "I really ought to go and see how things are getting on, sir."

Farnley looked at Roger. "Is there anything else you need Mr. Carmichael for?"

Roger said, "Nothing now, thanks." He didn't appear to watch as Carmichael went out, but he didn't miss the nondescript little man's eagerness to go.

"Mr. West," said Farnley briskly, "I don't want you to misunderstand me, but if we should get a hold-up now, even a trifling one, it could disrupt all of our Christmas posting arrangements. That apart, I'll do anything at all that I can to help. Anything. So will my staff."

"Yes, I'm sure," Roger said formally. "Thank

you. Detective Inspector Turnbull will be in charge when I'm not here."

"Good," said Farnley. "Good." Obviously, he hoped they would soon go.

Once they were out of the Postmaster's room, Turnbull said roundly: "Cold shoulder's not in it. And that Chief Sorter, Carmichael, puts up a funny act, doesn't he? Edgy as a monkey with a fleas."

He's probably haunted by thoughts of a parcels hold-up," Roger said. "Better have someone tag him, though."

He left Turnbull, and soon slid his car onto the Embankment; from here, he could be in his office in five minutes. In ten seconds under the five, he was getting out of his car.

A uniformed man from the top of the steps leading to the C.I.D. building came hurrying down.

"Mind you don't slip," Roger said. "There's frost on the steps."

"I'll be careful, sir, thanks," the duty sergeant said. He was breathing heavily. "A word in your ear, sir. There's a boy up here—lad of about eighteen, just raring to go. Says he must see you, won't be put off with anyone else. Shall I get rid of him?"

"Did he give a name?"

"Name of Bryant—and so young he ought to be in crawlers, not in uniform."

"I'll see him," said Roger, and began to hurry up the steps.

He'd already met Derek; this would be Micky Bryant.

4

Micky Bryant

The youth coming swiftly toward Roger might have risen from that cold stone slab after shedding thirty years of his age. Obviously he was in such distress that he hardly knew what he was doing. He pushed past the sergeant, who said sharply: "Now, I've warned you once."

"It's all right," said Roger. "If I'd just learned that my father had been murdered, I'd be pretty mad."

Micky Bryant stopped moving. Then his lips began to work and his eyes screwed up. He tried to speak, but couldn't. He was short for his age — over eighteen, or he wouldn't be in the Army.

"Let's get along to my room," Roger said, and walked briskly toward the lift. Bryant still didn't speak as they went up, then along the wide, bare corridors to Roger's office. His desk, one of five, was in a corner with a window overlooking the Embankment, the floodlit London County Hall, and the shimmering reflection of the lamps of Westminster Bridge on the Thames.

No one else was here.

"Sit down for half a minute, will you?" asked Roger, and pushed up a small green armchair. He himself sat on a corner of the desk and lifted a telephone—one of three on the desk. "Give me Sergeant Appleby, please." Brown trilby tipped to the back of his head, overcoat collar turned up, he looked vigorous, and right on top of his job. "Hallo, Appleby?...Just make a note of these things, will you, all to do with the Post Office investigation."

He saw Micky Bryant stiffen.

"...see that I get photographs of that footprint and a copy of the plaster cast," Roger said. "Have a word with the River Police and ask them—"

He broke off.

"You've *got* it?" he exclaimed. "Fine—yes, I'll be here. Anything else?...All right, thanks."

He put down the receiver, and looked keenly into the youth's face.

"Micky," he said, "I think you like it straight from the shoulder." The boy nodded. "Right. The River Police have found a weapon which they think was used to kill your father. That means we've made a good start. We've also found a footprint which will probably help to identify the killer. And there are fifty or so detectives ready to work night and day until they've found the man."

He stopped.

Micky Bryant said, slowly, gratingly: "That—that's what I came to—to see you about. You *must* find him."

"I think we shall."

"You *must* find him," the lad repeated, as if he hadn't heard the response. "It's the most terrible thing that's ever happened. My father was such a *good* man." Tears shimmered in the stricken eyes. "If I knew who it was, I'd kill him myself, the devil. I'd make sure he didn't live to kill anyone else."

Roger tipped his hat further back, and spoke very quietly.

"Listen, Micky. The law exists to punish murderers. If you found and killed this man, you'd be guilty of murder in the eyes of the law. How would that help your mother?"

All the boy could do was stare.

"Your job's to help us," Roger went on, more briskly. "Have you any idea at all who killed your father?"

"No, I only wish—"

"Just answer my questions. Have you any idea why he was killed?"

The boy shouted: "Of course I haven't!"

"All right, I had to ask. Derek's older than you, isn't he?"

"Yes, he's twenty-two."

"All your other brothers and sisters are younger, aren't they?"

"Yes much—much younger."

"Thanks. do you know where Derek's fiancée lives?"

"Oh, yes. She has a flat in Chelsea, 27 Barton Mews."

"Good," said Roger, and lit a cigarette. "Now, when were you last on leave?"

"It was only three weeks ago; now I'm on embarkation leave. I—excuse me, sir, do you think I shall get compassionate leave all right? I—I *must* stay at home with Mum."

"I think I can guarantee it," Roger said. "Don't

worry about that. You saw your father on your last leave, of course."

"Oh, yes. He took a day off, and we went—"

The boy broke off, and had to fight the tears. Roger looked down at the papers on his desk, and asked: "Did he say anything to suggest that he had any enemies?"

"Heavens, no! Everyone liked him." Micky's voice broke again.

"Did he say anything at all about his work?"

"Well—well, last night he said that things were really getting heavy, this time of the year is always the—the busiest in the Post Office, you know. He—he said he expected to have to work overtime every night, but didn't mind because it meant a little extra money for Mum." Micky caught his breath. *Oh, God, why did he have to die,?*"

Roger let the cry fade into silence, then asked quietly: "He held a pretty responsible position, didn't he?"

"Well—well, yes, in a way," Micky mumbled now. "He was a senior sorter."

"Parcels and letters?"

"Yes."

"Did that include registered post?"

"Oh, yes," said Micky, "I know it did. He took me round the new office the time before the last time I was on leave, with Mr. Farnley's permission, and showed me what they do with the registered parcels and letters. There'd been so much trouble."

Roger said: "That's what I'm getting at, Micky. There's been a lot of trouble with Post Office van robberies, and I wondered if your father ever suggested that he knew who was behind them."

"Oh, no!"

33

"Then that couldn't be the motive, could it? I suppose he hadn't won a fortune on the pools, or betting."

"Dad gamble? He'd rather starve!"

Then where had he got that hundred pounds?

"Wise man," Roger said briskly. "Now, I'll send you to my home, where you can join your mother, and go home with her. Do you know if she has any sisters, or anyone who'll come and stay with her?"

"Oh, May will. May's *won*derful."

"Good. What's her other name?"

"Rosemary."

Roger was surprised into a smile. "No, I mean her surname."

"Oh, I see. Harrison, May Harrison."

"Thanks. Has she known Derek for long?"

"Oh, yes, *years*."

"And what does Derek do for a living?"

They were at the lift by then.

"He works at River Way, too," said Micky Bryant. "He's on the maintenance side, mostly engineering. I don't really know what he does, except that it's mostly outside work." He stepped into the lift as Roger motioned him ahead. "May's like one of the family; it'll help a lot just to have her around."

"That's fine," said Roger, and meant it.

A few minutes later he watched the lad being driven off; then he went straight back to his office.

There was nothing at all to suggest that the murder might be connected with Bryant's private life; it seemed more likely to be connected with his work. In his humble way, he had been a key worker, handling a good proportion of the registered letters and parcels which went through

34

River Way. There had been dozens of Post Office van robberies in recent years, and some evidence that an inside worker was supplying the thieves with advance information. When the thieves knew where valuable packets would be coming from, and what time they were expected at the post offices, their task was easier.

Turnbull was already busy on that angle, consulting with officers of the Post Office Investigations Branch.

By working into the early hours, Roger could make up the time he had lost with the Bryant family.

He looked through some reports on a dozen other cases, and made notes for morning action, mostly delegated. His main job would be the Post Office murder, and he wanted to soak himself in the details.

A telephone bell rang.

He lifted the right receiver. "West speaking."

"What-ho, Handsome," said Detective Inspector Turnbull. His deep, powerful voice held a note of excitement. "I've picked up a bit of dope on our pal Carmichael, the Chief Sorter. He's got a bit of blonde stuff tucked away. Expensive piece, too—diamond earrings and bells on her toes. Now where would our Carmy get the money for high life like that?"

"Sure about this?" Roger demanded.

"Been seen by two P.O. detectives, night clubs and expensive restaurants."

"Have 'em both watched, but don't let them know about it yet. Could Carmichael be the killer?" Roger couldn't imagine the little man having the physical strength to deliver those terrible blows.

"No," said Turnbull, "he was in the office at the time; we couldn't pin the job on to him. But a Post Office chap with a salary of nine hundred a year keeping a blonde whose house rent must be five or six pounds a week smells high, doesn't it?"

"Couldn't smell much higher. Anything else come in at the River Way Post Office?"

"Nothing worth singling out. I'll make a report for the morning," Turnbull promised. "I hear they've found the instrument."

"They think they have."

Roger rang off, frowning, picked up a file of reports, but hadn't read the first one when the door opened and a bald-headed man looked in. It was going to be like this, with hardly a minute's peace.

"That hammer used on Bryant's come in," the man announced. "Coming up to see it?"

5

Hammer

Wilberforce, second in command of Fingerprints at the Yard, was short for a policeman, thin, straggly, with a monkeylike face and pouting lips and a constant tone of complaint; he was worked too hard, he was always on nights, there wasn't room in his little office, everyone wanted his particular job done first. This was the strain in which he talked as he went along, a pace behind Roger, toward the office. The door was marked with one word, Fingerprints, and opened onto a long, narrow room. A bench ran the whole length, with strip lighting immediately above it. At one end was a camera, standing on a wheeled tripod, and a small-sized movie screen; at the other was a movie projector and a color transparency projector. At intervals along the bench stood small boxes of gray powder, camel's-hair brushes and dusters; fastened to the walls, racks of tools. In one corner was a heap of rubbish; bottles, glasses, old handbags, tins, cigarette boxes, shoes, gloves—these and a hundred other things, all of them having one factor in common: smears of gray powder. These were the articles brought here and tested and then rejected, not being needed in court, and having no known owner.

In a glass case was the department's prized exhibit—the skin of a human hand, preserved for years, which had been so affected by immersion in water for some weeks that the police had been able to pull it off like a glove. The natural oils had been gone long since but the papillary lines had remained clear and, from the perfect prints recorded, the dead man had been identified.

Wilberforce had performed the whole operation.

A man, younger and much livelier-looking than Wilberforce, was holding a hammer in a large pair of calipers, which gripped it halfway along the wooden shaft. It was a long handle, and would lend plenty of power to a blow. The thick end of the head was shiny, the thin end was dull. The handle itself was a pale brown, and had once been varnished. The big young man had a small camera on the desk, and every now and again he picked it up and took a picture.

"What've you got?" asked Wilberforce.

"Couple of fragments; it hadn't been in the water long enough to spoil everything," said the young man promptly. He recognized Roger, and seemed to spring to attention. "Fragments of thumb and forefinger prints on the handle if the position of the fragments has been correctly estimated. Both impressions may be classified as tented arch pattern. I have photographed each from three separate angles and have requested development of prints at the earliest possible moment."

38

He stopped, almost breathlessly.

Wilberforce said dryly: "So you have. Finished with that hammer?"

"Yes, sir."

Wilberforce picked it up, swung it cautiously, grimaced, and handed it to Roger. Roger had to tense his muscles in order to lift it high enough for a blow. Anyone who could use this was either exceptionally strong in the forearm or had had plenty of practice.

"Cold chisel hammer," he said. "Anyone who wants to knock a hole in a wall might use it, a plumber or gas engineer or—"

''Trades by the dozen," Wilberforce put in. "Any handyman would have one of these; it doesn't mean a thing. Wonder how long those prints will be?"

The door opened.

"Anyone here awake?" asked a plump man, as he came in casually. He carried what looked like a thick sheet of blotting paper, damp on both sides. "Got some prints of prints, if you know what I mean, and they *did* say they're in a hurry."

"Lemme see," said Wilberforce, and grabbed.

The prints were inside the blotting paper, damp and dull. He put them on the bench, handling them carefully; they had been enlarged so that the fragments of the fingerprints were about the size of an average index finger tip—rather more than half an inch in diameter. Roger took a small magnifying glass from the rack on the wall, and peered at them. One was larger than the other; the ridges between the papillary lines were thicker, and it was almost possible to believe that they were the prints of two different men. They were roughly the same shape, the series of ridges shaped rather like bell tents of diminishing size.

On the larger of the two, the thumb, there was a small scar.

Wilberforce was examining the other print as closely.

"Well, if that's the hammer that was used on Bryant, those prints could hang the guy," he said. "Charlie."

"Yes, sir?" exclaimed the big young man.

"Take these up to Records, and see if we've got a dossier on the gentleman."

"Yes, sir." Charlie sped out. The other large man who had brought the prints grinned, and said:

"Little Hitler Wilberforce."

"Thanks, the pair of you," Roger said, and went out, along to the lift and up to the next floor; the laboratory floor.

The laboratory fascinated him as much as any place at the Yard, and was almost the only place where he felt out of his depth. The man in charge was named Dyson, short, thick-set, tough, a Yorkshireman with a face like an angry bulldog. He had several younger men on duty; the main laboratory was a throbbing mass of retorts and burettes, bubbling flasks and burning Bunsens. Dyson was in a smaller room, where there were three microscopes, and as Roger entered Dyson said:

"After that hammer report?"

"Please."

"Some people have the luck," said Dyson. "If it had been in the river much longer I doubt if we'd have found anything, but there was a bit. Blood Group O. Some was in a crack in the hammer head, and we scraped it out. Look." He touched a cellophane envelope which had white paper stuck on one side; some tiny fragments of something that looked like dried paint showed against the white. "Some was between the hammer head and the shaft—incidentally, when you get that hammer have a good look at the place where the wooden shaft goes into the head. Been altered to fit, and I should say it had been made smaller with a blunt knife. Amateur or emergency job."

"Fine, thanks," Roger said. "What about the blood spots found on the wall at Goose Lane, and on the footprint?"

"Both Group O." Dyson bared his small teeth. "But don't jump to any conclusions, Handsome; remember it's the biggest group."

"No other group on the hammer or the wall?"

"No."

"Thanks."

"You're welcome," Dyson said.

It was building up. It might crack quickly, too, if Records had those prints. It was almost too much to hope for, but they had over a million thumbprints and as many index fingerprints to choose from. Roger went back to his own desk, and wrote brief reports. Then he wrote an instruction for Turnbull to find out if a hammer was missing from the Post Office stores. As he finished, the telephone bell went.

"West speaking."

"Sergeant Green of Fingerprints here, sir," said the big young man. "I regret to report that Records has no record of the prints from the hammer shaft, sir."

"Oh. Pity. But thanks."

"Thank you, sir."

No record, mused Roger disappointedly; no short cut.

He arranged for a detective officer to go and relieve Sergeant Kilby at Clapp Street, and then sat back to ponder.

He wanted news of anyone who had seen a man leaving Goose Lane that evening, and a radio and television request could help, but he would need high authority for that—from the Assistant Commissioner for Crime. He knew that the A.C., Sir Guy Chatworth, was at a dinner at the Mansion House and wouldn't exactly appreciate it if he were disturbed.

Couldn't be helped.

Roger picked up a telephone, and asked for the *Daily Globe* News Room. He hadn't long to wait.

"Is Larry Graham there?" he asked.

"Who wants him?"

"West of Scotland Yard."

There was a chuckle. "He'll be in. *Larry!* Handsome West wants to bleed you dry." A pause, and then a low-pitched, lazy-sounding voice came to Roger's ears. "That wouldn't be Chief Inspector West in person, would it?"

"Larry," said Roger, "I want just a trifling piece of information and help, and I've nothing to offer in return, but think how important our good will is. You're covering the Mansion House banquet tonight, aren't you?"

"Yes. Pooh-Bah is talking."

"What time is the reception over?"

"Eight-fifteen. That's nearly now."

"Call your man," asked Roger. "Ask him to find Chatworth and delay him for a few minutes. I

42

want to get the old man before he goes in to the meal, it'll be a waste of time trying afterward."

Larry said: "Who'm I to throw a reporter to the coppers? Okay."

It took Roger ten minutes to reach the Mansion House, where his card won him a way past the flunkeys on duty. It was a semi-public function, with the Lord Mayor in the chair and a two-hour meal to follow the reception; and after that, politicians' speeches.

Roger reached a doorway leading to the great room where dinner was to be served. There was a little ante-room close by, and Chatworth was standing and looking down at a man who scarcely reached as high as his chin.

Roger blessed all news-room men.

"Sorry to interrupt you, sir." This was a time to be formal. He saw Chatworth start and look round. The A.C. had a mighty paunch and a round, red face, grizzled hair which was like a halo, and a weather-beaten bald patch. His tail suit was a little too small for him, and he wore many decorations.

"What the devil do *you* want?"

"Sorry, sir," said Roger, "it couldn't wait. The postman murder; you heard about it just before you left. I've checked all the angles, and the one you suggested is the most likely."

"Oh." Chatworth put his head on one side, and didn't smile. The other guests had gone in, and a man's voice was raised:

"*Gentlemen, please receive your President, the Right Honorable...*" "And what angle did *I* think up?"

"Still no reason to think that this murder had a

43

private motive," Roger said, "and Bryant held a subordinate but key position in River Way Post Office. I think it's big enought to turn on all the heat we can. We've the hammer—the weapon used—prints—and a footprint. What we need is an eyewitness who saw the killer leave Goose Lane, and if we put the request over through the B.B.C. . . ."

Chatworth didn't lose a second.

"All right. But the Controller of the British Broadcasting Corporation is also here. I advise you not to apply the same tactics to him."

Roger grinned.

Chatworth turned away.

"*. . . who will say grace,*" the toastmaster was intoning.

"How much of that stuff can I use?" asked Dawson, the *Globe* man, eagerly. "I mean about the hammer, prints—"

"All of it."

"Be a pal and run me back to the office," pleaded the newspaperman. "There's never a cab in the city at this time of night. You can phone Broadcasting House and Lime Grove from there, too."

"All right, but get a move on," Roger said.

Roger spent half an hour at Scotland Yard, checking everything that had come in. A telephoned report on his desk said that Chief Sorter Carmichael was in his love nest; there was also a report saying that Carmichael was a widower, and the association with the blonde was about six months old.

Roger finished the chores at half past ten. He

went down to Information Room, where the inevitable tension of the night was noticeable; patrol-car models were being pushed around on the big tables, half a dozen men were at telephones or radio telephones, several tape recording machines were turning.

"Anything we can do for you?" asked the inspector in charge.

"Nothing in from the broadcasts?"

"Not a thing."

"Oh, well," said Roger. "No false alarms, anyhow." He checked with the main switchboard and got the same reply, then went up to his car and drove along the Embankment toward his home in Bell Street, Chelsea. So, he had to pass the mammoth G.P.O. building. The top floors were in darkness, but the ground floor and several above it were ablaze with light. Vans were swinging in and out of the main entrance in quick succession. He caught a glimpse of one of the loading platforms and the chutes which swallowed up the parcels. Christmas presents on the way to the world at large—and the great office was a man short.

Roger drove on.

At the corner of Bell Street, five youths were gathering about a doorway. Their singing sounded above the sound of the engine. *While shepherds watched their flocks by night*. Three doors from his own house, there was a lighted Christmas tree already in the window.

The hall light was on in Roger's house.

He put the car into the narrow drive but not into the garage itself, and went in, closing the door quietly. He heard dance music coming from the radio, and Janet humming. Resilient creatures, human beings. He whistled, and Janet looked up from the kitchen table, which seemed to be a mass of empty dishes, empty packets, bits and pieces; and in the center was the big brown mixing bowl half filled with a sticky-looking mixture which smelled good.

"Oh, good!" greeted Janet. "I was going to give you five more minutes and then put them in the basins, but I do like everyone to stir the puddings." She handed him the sticky wooden spoon, then licked her own finger. "And, darling, pop up and see if the boys are asleep yet. Scoop won the championship tonight. He's so thrilled, and Richard's almost as pleased."

"I'll go up," Roger promised, and stirred. He was delighted at the news. "Good old Scoop!" The thick, sticky mixture was much harder to stir than he had expected; it was every year. But this was the first year that he thought of a heavy hammer, also hard to lift and difficult to wield.

"Oh, don't take a week of Sundays," Janet scoffed, "I don't know who started the rumor that men are the stronger sex. Let me—"

"No, I'll make a job of it. Did young Micky Bryant come here?"

Janet said, in a quieter voice: "I thought that would get on your mind. Yes. They were both very —well, brave, I suppose. *Let me do that.* I left them alone for a little while, and the boy was full of what you'd told him and what you were doing. *Let me have it.*" She wrenched the spoon away, and then pointed it at him, aggressively. "I often wonder why it's so difficult to say this kind of thing, Roger, but I think you saved that boy from going mad. Now *look!* Get the spoon well down

46

and twist." She handed him back the spoon. "And *don't spill half of it on the floor.*"

Roger gave a few quick turns, took the spoon out, licked the mixture off the end, and said: "Not enough carrots," and went out.

Well, there were grounds for rejoicing. Martin called Scoopy was his school's boxing champion; a triumph. He could imagine the boys had lain awake for hours hoping that he would be home in time to be told. Now—

He opened their door, and heard their even breathing.

"Anyone awake?" he whispered.

There was no answer.

He went downstairs, and into the front room. It was getting a little shabby, but had the homely look which mattered. His armchair, with the winged back to the window, was drawn up in front of the electric fire, and on a table by its side was whiskey, a syphon of soda, a glass, his pipe and tobacco; he liked a pipe in the evening. He went to a small writing bureau, took out a sheet of paper and printed in high letters: *Hi, champ!* and left that on top of the bureau, to take upstairs later. Then he poured himself a drink and sat down to relax with it. He was halfway through, thinking more of the boys and of Janet than of the Bryants, when he heard the click of the kitchen light.

Janet reached this door. It was nearly midnight, and she looked very tired.

The telephone bell rang.

"Oh, bother," she said, but it wasn't with the vexation she usually showed toward late calls.

The telephone was near Roger's chair.

"Let me say you're out," Janet suggested, half-heartedly.

Roger grimaced at her, as he picked the receiver up. "West speaking."

"Kilby here, sir," said Sergeant Kilby, a little too loudly. "Thought you'd want to know that two people have turned up in answer to the television request. They were walking on the Embankment just after five o'clock tonight, and saw a chap hurrying out of Goose Lane. Instead of telephoning, they came straight to the Yard."

"Hold 'em," said Roger promptly. "I'll be there." He put the receiver down, finished his drink, and then slid an arm round Janet's waist. "You go to bed, sweetheart, and don't pretend you're not longing to get tucked in. I won't be long."

"You'll probably be all night," said Janet, lugubriously. "Is it about the Bryant murder?"

"Yes."

"You can go," Janet said.

He kissed her; drew back; kissed her again. Then he turned away quickly, and went out into the chilly night.

It would take him only ten minutes to get to the Yard through the empty streets.

6

Eyewitnesses

Kilby was in the front hall to meet Roger, the light showing him to be a big, hearty and hardy-looking man.

"They're in the waiting room," he greeted. "Seem a straightforward pair." They began to walk toward the lift. "The boy's in the River Way Post Office, wages section, and the girl's at one of the big stores—it's her half-day. He's an early-turn worker, should have been through at three o'clock but all the staff is doing overtime, so he arranged to meet girl friend just after five."

"Thanks," said Roger. "Did they get a good view of the chap?"

Kilby gave a snort of a laugh.

"They wouldn't tell me anything, said that they would only talk to the officer in charge."

He opened the door of one of the waiting rooms.

The young couple would probably be lost in any crowd, but at close quarters the character in the boy's face showed up; and the girl had a common-sense look about her.

"Good evening," greeted Roger. "Very good of you to come here as late as this."

If they really knew anything, it was more than good, it was wonderful.

"Only too glad, if we can help," said the youth carefully, "but excuse me, you *are* the senior officer in charge of the case, aren't you?"

"I'm Chief Inspector West."

"Oh. That's good." The youth squeezed the girl's hand. "Only I wanted to make sure. Well, I'm speaking for us both, sir. We certainly saw a man hurry from Goose Lane across the road and throw something in the Thames and then go racing off on a motorcycle. It all happened very quickly. We—er—we were in a doorway, and no one else was about as far as I know."

"Did you recognize the man?" asked Roger.

"Well, we couldn't swear to it," the youth said. "What would you do if we did name someone?"

"We'd keep a close check on his movements," Roger said promptly, "and we'd try to make sure that you hadn't made a mistake. If we found out that he'd been somewhere else at the time—well, that would speak for itself."

"Arthur," said the girl unexpectedly, "I think you ought to to tell him."

The lad looked grave; as if he felt a heavy burden of responsibility.

"As a matter of fact," he said at last, "it was a fellow named Wilson. I don't know him very well. He's one of the temporary workers we take on during the Christmas rush. We always have a few for several weeks before Christmas; the overseas mail starts getting very heavy then, both ways. Wilson was one of the first temporaries, sir. I know, because I help to make up the wages."

"Did you get a really good look at him?" asked Roger, and felt a fierce glow of excitement.

"Oh, yes, under one of the lamps. At first we saw him running; in fact he looked as if he was going under a lorry. Gave my fiancée quite a turn. We didn't recognize Wilson until he was close to the Embankment, and then—well, we're pretty sure that it was Wilson, but we couldn't absolutely swear to it."

"You've done wonders," Roger said. "Can't give me his full name and address, can you?"

"I'm ever so sorry, I can't," the lad said, "but it'll be at the office."

Work at the River Way Office was at a very low ebb when Roger arrived. It was a little after one o'clock. Two vans were being unloaded, and the parcels looked lost in the gaping maws of the chutes. The wide, clean-looking loading and unloading platforms were almost deserted. All the men on duty wore uniforms, except the driver of a van who wore ordinary clothes with a band round his left arm, marked ER. Roger went upstairs, not taking the lift, and into the huge letter-sorting office. That afternoon this had been thick with men handling letters. Now, it was nearly empty. Round the walls were thousands upon thousands of pigeonholes, each clearly marked, and every pigeonhole had its quota of letters. In regular lines running the full length of the room were letter racks, none standing very high; more letters were in these. One corner of the room was occupied by workers, near the main doors. Also near here were hundreds of big sacks fitted inside special stands,

51

so that the mouths of the sacks were held wide open. These were for small parcels, or packets.

A little gray-haired man with ruddy cheeks was in charge.

"Oh, yes, Inspector, very glad to help in any way I can. Terrible business, terrible. Your men are on the premises, of course. I'm sure I hope that you catch the murderer very soon. Now, what was it you needed? Names and addresses of the temporary workers? I can't tell you how glad I am to hear you say that; it would be awful to think that we had a murderer working among our regular staff, wouldn't it?" He would have sounded smug but for his bright little smile. "If you'll come with me to the office, I'll get the list." He meant the Chief Sorter's office, which was partitioned off in a corner of the room. Carmichael's desk was scrupulously tidy. "We keep a list of all the temporary workers, and make a note of their hours, and the time sheets go upstairs to the wages office once a week. Just like an ordinary business house, I suppose. Now, let me see, I expect Mr. Carmichael keeps it locked away." The little man jingled keys, opened a safe, pulled open the door and took out the time sheet. He spread this on a desk.

There was Wilson: *Aubrey Peter Wilson, 58 Niger Street, Shepherd's Bush, W.12.* He was the fourth on the list of temporaries, and thirty or forty names had been added since.

"It's a lucky thing you didn't want this tomorrow; we shall take on hundreds more," said the little man, earnestly.

"How are they selected?" Roger inquired.

"Well, we have to be satisfied that they are people of good repute, of course, but they have no responsibility beyond the actual letters and parcels they take out or collect, and they are usually watched—not with any intent, sir, it just happens that they're usually in twos. Even *threes*. The method of selection—well, it isn't easy to get spare-time workers in these days of full employment, but of course we get a quota from the Employment Exchange, and the moment the schools and colleges break up for the holiday we get a flood of young men—and girls, of course."

"Who signs them on?"

"Well, in fact the Chief Sorter does. It's not like selection for the permanent staff, you understand. Have you—ah—have you got everything you need?"

"May I have one of my men make a copy of this?" asked Roger.

"Oh, perfectly all right," breathed the little man. "Perfectly."

Roger went down to the stores and maintenance quarters, in the basement; three men from the Yard were working there, checking equipment and tools and questioning the one or two maintenance staff workers then on duty. It was a gloomy place, with several low, arched doorways leading to tunnels, now used as store rooms, which had once led down to the river. There was no report of a missing hammer.

Roger sent a man to copy out the time sheet, then arranged for a sergeant to meet him at the Shepherd's Bush station, and headed fast for West London, through the dark streets.

Fox-Wilkinson, in charge at Shepherd's Bush H.Q. by night, was one of the youngest senior Divisional officers, dark-haired, keen, spruce, ready to

take any short cut that offered. He had no information about an Aubrey Peter Wilson who lived at
58 Niger Street, but could soon call in the constable who did the street's night beat.

"Let's go to him," said Roger. "You can have my
sergeant sent ahead."

"I'll fix it." Fox-Wilkinson spoke to an inspector,
then led the way downstairs. "We'll go in your car,
shall we?" The whole London Force knew Roger's
preference for driving himself. "Keep on the way
you're heading, then third right," Fox-Wilkinson
directed, and added after a pause: "If this chap
Wilson knew anything about the postman job,
we'd better not take it too easily."

"We'll be careful," Roger said.

"Yes, sir, I know a bit about Wilson at Number
58," the police constable said. He was one of the
older, more solid types; five minutes with him told
the whole story of why he was still on the beat.
"Bit of a boxer, but never done very much—too
much talk and not enough training. Easy money,
that's what Wilson's always after. I've kept an eye
on him for some time. Does a bit of betting, passes
a few slips, I shouldn't wonder. Nasty piece of
work, if you ask me."

"Any reason for saying that?" asked Roger.

"Well—in a way. He had a quarrel with a pal,
after a dance at the Hammersmith Palais. Beat
him up pretty badly, but there wasn't anything we
could do about it. I'd be careful with Wilson, if I
was you; he's pretty tough. Why, I've seen him
bend an iron bar with his bare hands!"

"Oh, have you?" Roger said heavily.

"Got all you want?" asked Fox-Wilkinson.

"Yes, thanks. As soon as my man arrives, we'll go to the house. If you'll see that it's covered, back and front, I don't think we'll have much trouble with Wilson."

Roger waited alone in the car round the corner from Niger Street. First to arrive was Sergeant Kilby, in a patrol car; and, had he wanted it, Kilby could have been home in bed. They walked to the corner. The street lights were out and there were no lighted windows, but the stars were shining.

"Be a bit of all right if we catch the swine as quickly as this," said Kilby. "This job's done something to me." He was always economical with his "sirs." "As a matter of fact, it was that May Harrison who flattened me, the way it upset her, and the way she steadied the two brothers. Young Micky took it hard; the eldest boy, Derek, just seemed numb. Went off soon afterward, to tell his grandmother, I gather." Kilby was talking disconnectedly. "Just opened my eyes in a way I hadn't seen before. Nice family like that, broken wide open. Makes you feel that the dead chap isn't the one to be sorry for."

"I know just what you mean," said Roger. He heard footsteps, and recognized Fox-Wilkinson. "Everything ready?"

"Yes," the local man said. "But you can do me a favor. Let me come up with you. I know it's your show, but—"

"Come and welcome," said Roger.

They walked quietly along the unlit street, and as they drew toward Number 58, Roger shone a torch.

"Here we are," said Fox-Wilkinson. "We're bound to wake Wilson when we're knocking."

"If he cuts and runs for it we'll have a stronger case," said Roger, philosophically. He shone the torch on the door, and found a battery-type bell set in the middle. He rang twice, and then kept his finger on the push.

The jarring sound seemed to echo up and down the street.

Men on the other side of the road would be watching the top window, and men at the back would make sure that Wilson didn't get away.

He stopped, then rang again.

Suddenly there were footsteps inside; heavy thumping, as if on stairs, and steadier, shuffling sounds as someone came along the passage. Whoever it was fumbled with a key, there was a sharp click, then the door opened an inch and a man asked roughly: "What the hell do you want?"

"It's all right," Roger began, "we're police, and—"

"I don't give a damn who you are, waking up decent folk in the middle of the night! What—"

"Is Wilson in?"

There was a pause.

"So it's Wilson again," the man said, in a resigned voice. "It's the last night he sleeps here; there's been nothing but trouble since he came. Why, my own daughter isn't safe from him, he—"

Roger put his shoulder to the door, and pushed. The man backed hastily away. He was dressed in striped pajamas and a thick blue overcoat; his long nose was red, and he looked perished with cold.

"Where is he?" asked Roger curtly.

56

The bluster died away.

"Up-upstairs, the back room, he—but what do you want him for?"

"Just to ask him a few questions. We won't keep you up long."

Roger hurried to the head of the stairs and a narrow landing. A door stood wide open, and there was a light on in the room beyond. A woman called: "Perce, what is it?"

Roger turned toward the back rooms. He could make out the shape of a doorway but there was no light on in the room beyond. Wilson might be climbing out of the window, or might be crouching behind the door—possibly holding another weapon.

There was no sound.

Fox-Wilkinson was just behind Roger, now; the floor boards creaked. The man with the red nose was standing in the doorway of his bedroom. Roger put on the landing light. The door ahead was flimsy, and he could get it down with little trouble. He put his shoulder to it, and thrust with his whole weight.

The door crashed in.

There was only dark silence beyond.

7

Pattern of Events

Roger recovered his balance, halfway inside the room. By then the silence had lost its menace; if Wilson had been waiting to attack, he would have shown himself. There was nothing to suggest that he had got out of the window; in the light from the landing, it showed up clearly, and the curtains were drawn.

Roger thought: "So he's flown," and switched on the bedroom light—and stopped moving.

Wilson hadn't flown.

He lay on the bed, fully dressed, and the ugly thing was the gash at his throat; as ugly, the blood which must have drenched the bedclothes, and had now dried to a dark brown; there was hardly a touch of red. Wilson's knees were drawn up, in an oddly uncanny way; as a live man's. It looked as if he had been killed while lying on his back with his hands behind his neck and his legs drawn up.

Fox-Wilkinson said heavily: "Well, what about that?"

"Now I think we're beginning to see how big it

is," Roger said slowly. The first effect of the shock was easing off; it wouldn't take long to go. "Better get Wilberforce over here right away. Your chaps can look after the rest, can't they?"

"Glad to."

"Here, what's going on?" demanded the man with the red nose. He put up a show of bravado, and moved forward. "What's the game, is—"

"Come with me a minute, will you?" asked Roger, and gripped a bony wrist, making the man go with him into the room. One look at the bed, and the man made a retching sound. "Just tell me this," said Roger evenly. "Is that Wilson?"

"Y-y-y-yes," gabbled the landlord. "Let me get out of here, let me get out."

It didn't take long to get things moving. Divisional men took over the routine, a divisional police surgeon was on the spot within fifteen minutes, Wilberforce with his big assistant soon afterward.

Roger tackled the man and wife and their daughter. The family name was Evans, and the daughter seemed to be worth three of her parents, an alert, well-spoken brunette in her early twenties.

They'd heard Wilson come in, about half past ten, with someone else—they'd known it was a man because of his footsteps. The men had gone straight to Wilson's room and switched on the radio; he usually got a foreign station, with dance music. They hadn't heard anyone leave, but they'd been listening to their own radio.

The police could not find the weapon.

The doctor hadn't much doubt about it being a

long knife with a very sharp blade; there had been no hacking, just one sweeping blow.

The only new find of significance was a brown stain on one of Wilson's shoes—a shoe which might have made that impression in the mud at Goose Lane. Roger took this with him, and drove back to the yard. The laboratory night staff lost no time confirming that the brown stain was blood, and Roger soon found that the shoe matched the cast.

But there was still no answer to the vital questions. Had Wilson killed Bryant? Or had Wilson known the killer, and been killed because of what he could tell?

Roger set the Yard and the Divisions to work at high pressure, to trace all of Wilson's friends, and check and double-check his movements. Then he went back to Wilson's room, arriving as Wilberforce finished his first search.

"Looked for any prints yourself, Handsome?"

"Always leave that to the experts."

"You'd be a wiser man if you did! Well, take a look at these. And these and these and these." Wilberforce kept stabbing his finger about the room; at the electric switch, the door handle, the radio, at a cigarette case, at a glass, at a beer bottle. "Wilson's prints are all over the place, but they weren't on that hammer shaft."

That was a disappointment and reminded Roger of his earlier fears: there would be no short cut.

"Pity," he said.

Wilberforce grinned.

"Don't be downhearted! The man who handled that hammer's been here." Wilberforce showed him a print on a plain tumbler which smelled of whisky. "See? Been wiped, but he left a dab; too much of a hurry, I suppose. Tented arch and the little scar. Bit of luck we got that; the glass had a smear of fat on it—butter, I'd say—and there was the dab, large as life. Wilson was killed by the man who handled that hammer."

"Well, that's something," Roger said.

He left soon afterward, checked with the Yard, and was home and in bed just after four o'clock.

He didn't wake until half past ten next morning, and as soon as his eyes flickered open sensed that it was late. There was the broad daylight of winter brightness, sounds in the street which he was seldom at home to hear; and no sound in the house. He got up, opened the door and called:

"Anyone home?"

Janet didn't answer.

Roger yawned, rasped his chin, put on a dressing gown and went downstairs, calling Janet and getting no response. On the kitchen table was a note: *Gone to shops, back about eleven, A.C. said telephone him as soon as you're awake.* So Chatworth was on the ball. Roger put on a kettle and looked through the newspapers as he waited for it to boil. He was featured in several of them. Bryant's murder made the front pages in every newspaper—it had exactly the right news value, a Christmas story of *Murder in the Post Office.* Every newspaper took up the line that it might be connected with the Post Office robberies which had spread over many years.

The kettle boiled.

Roger made tea, letting it brew while he telephoned the Yard and asked for Chatworth. He reported, briefly, and Chatworth made no comment that mattered; he was not a man who talked for the sake of talking.

"Put me through to Turnbull's desk, sir, will you?" Roger asked.

Turnbull was soon on the line.

"Find out anything more about that hammer?" asked Roger.

"No, nothing at all," Turnbull said. "You had all the fun." Roger let that pass. "Carmichael turned up on the tick of eight, as usual, a stickler for punctuality. Any fresh orders?"

"No," said Roger. "I'll be seeing you."

He had two cups of tea, shaved, washed, dressed, and went downstairs as Janet arrived, fully laden. As she hustled about to get him some breakfast, she complained about the shops and the prices, and there was a sharper edge to her voice than usual. One of those mornings! The boys had been difficult to wake up, apparently; she'd been cross with them, and it was so vexing on the day that Scoopy was so happy about his triumph. Roger said: "Oh lor'," and went into the front room. There was his *Hi, champ!* on top of the writing desk just where he had left it last night. He took it up to the boys' room and left it on Scoopy's bed, and when he came down, breakfast was ready. Twenty minutes later, he gave Janet a peck of a kiss and left.

Nothing new had come in at the Yard.

Except for the one on the glass, the only fingerprints at Wilson's place were those of the unknown murderer, Wilson, and the Evans family—man, wife, and daughter.

Roger put in a written report, for Chatworth, and went along to the River Way Post Office.

As he turned into the big yard, he whistled.

It was crammed with vehicles, mostly Post Office red, but a few privately owned, nearly all dark colors. It swarmed with people, mostly men and mostly young. The heaps of parcels on the unloading and the loading platforms were mountainous. There was a kind of rhythm about the way everything was done, and yet the chutes were choked, and if the inflow of parcels increased, there wouldn't be room for them. He had never seen anything quite like it—and there, in the middle of the great piles of parcels, looking like a tiny dictator, was Carmichael.

He was directing the work.

Roger watched him for fully five minutes. Some men made a lot of fuss and got little done, some made no fuss and got everything done. That was Carmichael. He might be a slimy piece of work, but he was efficient, and his men jumped to his orders. Wherever the piles of parcels looked largest and the chutes were threatened with overloading, there was Carmichael—not striding, but pointing, speaking in a quiet voice, setting everything on the move.

Roger parked near the entrance, because there was no room further in the yard, and walked toward the loading platform. There were steps at intervals, where he could climb up. He didn't go to Carmichael, but saw Turnbull just inside the huge sorting room.

"Hallo, Handsome," he greeted. "What do you think of our overseer?" He was just too familiar, but Roger let it pass.

"He's doing quite a job."

"He's so busy that he hasn't time to give us

63

much help this morning, and Farnley is saying that if we interfere too much it will choke the whole works," Turnbull said. "Wants to know whether we can't postpone questioning Carmichael until the flood's slackened a bit, or he's having his lunch. Apparently they've had four ships in together at Southampton, all held up by the gales, and this is the result. Chaos, and—"

"Better leave Carmichael for a bit," Roger said; "if we get their backs up it isn't going to help. Any news of that hammer?"

Turnbull said: "Yes," in a way that puzzled Roger.

"Whose?"

"Maintenance engineer. Some weeks ago he lent it to another maintenance engineer, name Bryant. Derek Bryant."

Roger echoed: "*Derek* Bryant?" unbelievingly.

"That's it," said Turnbull. "And young Bryant's been in this morning—he didn't take the morning off."

"Where is he now?" asked Roger, sharply.

"Out on a job—there's been a bit of trouble at one of the sub Post Offices. Pipe burst or something. I didn't find out about the hammer until he'd left. I've got the number of his motorcycle, and we can put a call out for him—"

"Not yet," Roger said.

When you had been in the force as long as he had, you didn't rule out any possibility, but this—

Well, they could soon tackle Derek Bryant.

He heard a shout outside, so clear above the general hubbub that he turned quickly away from Turnbull, and went to the loading platform. He saw Carmichael standing in a little oasis of platform space and surrounded by the parcels, and a big, burly man in a postman's uniform.

"I tell you I didn't leave the van for ten seconds," this man roared, "never mind ten minutes!"

Everyone nearby had stopped working; for a moment, the parcels hardly seemed to matter. The postman was a head taller than the Chief Sorter, and was clenching his fists; but Carmichael looked him up and down without any sign of nervousness, and said in an incisive voice:

"You must have left your van, Simm."

"I tell you I didn't!"

"Then perhaps you can explain why three sealed, registered bags are missing," Carmichael said, coldly. "They were there, you've reported that yourself, and it's in your record book, and they're *not* there now."

"They must be."

"Very well," said Carmichael, "go and look for yourself." He put a hand to the postman's arm and led him a few yards along the platform; there was a small red van, open at the back, with two men guarding it. Now everyone in the yard had stopped working, and the silence was startling.

Turnbull was just behind Roger.

"Now we'll see fun," he said. "Now we'll see if Mr. Ruddy Carmichael can find time for us."

"Hold it," Roger said.

"Simm," said Carmichael in the same incisive way, "you had better lock the door of your van, and—"

Roger was on the move.

"Mind if I have a look at the van first?" he said, and didn't wait for an answer. Carmichael gave the impression that he would have refused if he could. Instead, he nodded and then called out to the absorbed, watching men: "What's the matter, have you forgotten that Christmas is coming?" He got them busy again, and the chutes soon filled up.

Roger went with Simm to the van.

"I tell you I didn't leave the van for a minute," the postman insisted. "I've been on this job for twenty years; think I don't know a thing or two? I wouldn't leave my van unlocked whether I had registers in or not, and you can take it from me— but who the hell are *you?*"

Roger said: "From the Yard, here on the Bryant job."

"Perishin' copper," Simm said, as if the news had done him good. "Take it from me if they set the dogs on me, I'll have them for defamation of character. *I*'ve done *my* job." he pointed to the back of the van, where two men stood as if on guard. It was stacked to the top with sacks of parcels, and the only gap was just at one side. "That's where they were, all flipping three of them. Sealed, too. And I didn't leave the van—"

"For a flipping minute. I heard you."

Simm grinned.

"Okay, okay, we understand each other! Well, look for yourself. See if that lock's been tampered with."

Roger said dryly: "Thanks."

The double doors at the back of the van were made of heavy steel. The lock was a modern Landon, and would take a lot of forcing; there was no sign at all that it had been forced. A few scratches on the outside had almost certainly been made with the keys.

"Well?" asked Simm, aggressively.

"Who has the key to this?"

"Strike a flipping light, what a question! I have." Simm took a bunch of keys from beneath his coat, and shook them. "That's it." He singled one key out, and pushed it in front of Roger's nose.

"Anyone else?"

"There's a duplicate key in the office, and the master key which Mr. Fli—"

"Skip the description."

Simm grinned again. He had good white teeth, and knew it.

"Okay, *Mr.* Carmichael has a master key."

"Who has access to it?"

"*Mr.* Carmichael, or the Postmaster. It's like asking to look at the Crown Jewels to get permission to use that key."

"Hm." Roger turned to Turnbull. "Call the Yard, have someone out here from Fingerprints to check that van all over."

"If you think you're going to take my dabs—" Simm began.

Roger said casually, "Oh, we won't do that until you're under arrest," and moved away. Simm gaped after him. Turnbull grinned, jumped down, and hurried to the car, to radio the Yard. Two policemen had come up from the sorting office itself, and Roger left them to watch the van. Simm followed him.

Ten minutes had worked a kind of miracle with the parcels, and Carmichael stood calm and detached in the middle of the few that were left. No man ever looked less like a mouse.

"Now if you can spare a few minutes," Roger said, "we'd better report this to the Postmaster."

"That has been done," retorted Carmichael, "I

had a message sent to him. Simm, I want you to go over your movements this morning very carefully; you will find that you did leave the van for a few minutes at some place or other. And—"

Simm raised two big, clenched fists.

"Listen," he roared in a foghorn voice, "you might be the Chief Sorter, you might be the Shah of Persia, but you don't get away with calling *me* a liar. I didn't leave my van for ten seconds without locking it. Gawd! With the pillar boxes crammed full you take five minutes to empty one."

"Let us see the Postmaster," said Carmichael, coldly. He motioned Simm to go ahead, and then spoke quietly to Roger, more human than he had yet shown himself. "It is much more difficult to trace the source of trouble at Christmas time. This can be extraordinarily difficult. It could be disastrous to the smooth running of Her Majesty's mails."

He said that as if robberies as robberies didn't matter; only the job was important.

Roger said: "We needn't start jumping our fences," and walked on toward the lift.

The Postmaster was as harassed as Carmichael, and a glimpse of the seeming chaos in the Sorting Room and the fantastic stacks of mail made it easy to understand. There was little that Roger could do here now, but he waited until Wilberforce's men arrived, and went over Simm's van.

There were dozens of prints of the same man; Simm's.

On the lock, there was a fragment of a print— identical with that found on the hammer and on the glass in Wilson's room.

"We'll see how far this gets us," Roger said. "It

won't be long before we have to take the dabs of everyone working at River Way."

He meant it; but he knew it would run him into trouble and conflict. The permanent staff was over a thousand, and there were as many temporary workers. That was bad enough. Carmichael's and Farnley's screams of protest would make it worse. They'd pull every string they had to stop it.

The police found nothing else to help on the van. Simm stuck to his story.

Turnbull had finished all the routine work at the Post Office and reported that Derek Bryant hadn't yet returned.

"I think it's time we questioned him about that hammer," he said.

Roger was crisp.

"Yes, get hold of him and do that, but keep it to yourself until you've seen me again."

"Okay," said Turnbull.

Roger went back to the Yard. He soon telephoned Chatworth and told him he wanted to take the fingerprints of all the River Way employees, and he guessed from the A.C.'s cool reaction that Chatworth also anticipated trouble.

"Any other time I'd say go ahead," he said, "but I'd better talk to the Postmaster General first. Can it wait until tomorrow?"

"I suppose it can," Roger said. "But today would be better."

"I'll see what I can do," promised Chatworth.

Roger busied himself with reports and snippets of news about this and a dozen other jobs, and was sorting them out when the telephone rang. He had a sneaking hope that Chatworth had fixed the

P.M.G. already, but this was a sergeant who was working with Turnbull.

"Handsome, here's a do." the sergeant greeted him, and something in his tone stopped the "Handsome" from being familiar. "Derek Bryant's skipped. He left the job he was out on but hasn't come back."

Derek Bryant wasn't found, that day, in spite of the widespread search.

Mrs. Bryant seemed too numbed to feel any more, but May Harrison's self-control almost snapped under the new strain.

Young Micky was wild-eyed, but outwardly calm.

By noon next day, there was still no fresh news. Roger checked and double-checked, wearied himself with a mass of reports, and found it difficult to concentrate on any but the Post Office murder. He was through the morning's reports, just after twelve o'clock, when the telephone bell rang.

"West," he said briskly.

"Better get over to Clapp Street, quick," said Turnbull harshly. "There's more trouble at the Bryants' place."

8

The Bryants' Place

A little before five o'clock on the morning after Derek Bryant had disappeared, Mrs. Bryant allowed May and Micky to persuade her to go upstairs, at least to lie down. They had talked through this second frightening, lonely night, saying the same thing over and over again, reviving the old hurts without knowing what they were doing. Mrs. Bryant's face was as colorless as it had been after she had first been told. Micky, who talked more than any of them, was looking better. May Harrison had just let them talk, had made tea, had made them eat a sandwich or two.

None of the other children yet knew their father was dead, only that he was missing. And now Derek—

"Of course, I'll have to tell the children myself, sooner or later," Mrs. Bryant said. "I don't know how I'm going to do it, but I'll have to go through with it somehow." She raised her hands from her knees, and dropped them again. "It isn't the kind of job that I can leave to anyone else, is it?"

"Mum, dear, why don't you try to get some rest?" May pleaded.

"Yes, I suppose you're right," Mrs. Bryant said, "although how I'm going to rest, with Dad and Derek—oh, it can't have happened to him, too!"

May said stiffly: "Please don't talk like that. Have two of these tablets the doctor gave you."

"I don't want to drug myself into forgetfulness," Mrs. Bryant said crossly. "I—oh, I don't know what I do want! May, I really don't know."

"Of course you don't," May said. "But come up-stairs now."

"Yes, Mum, you ought to," Micky urged.

"I suppose I'd better," Mrs. Bryant said again, and stood up.

Micky went up with her, and May Harrison stayed in the kitchen. There was little sign of the party now, although some of the holly was still up, and a few of the festoons.

The younger children were in the two small bed-rooms upstairs, two boys and a girl. Nine, seven, and three. Well, the toddler wouldn't feel much. Nine, seven and three. And—where was Derek? May felt her eyes stinging, and doused her face in cold water. The kettle was singing. She turned the gas up, filled a hot-water bottle, and then put two tablets from a small box into the saucer with a cup of milk; she would heat the milk for Mrs. Bryant in the bedroom.

May went toward the stairs.

Micky, on the landing, looked as if he was ready to drop. His eyes were red-rimmed and glassy, his lips were strained. He'd had little sleep the previous night, none yet tonight, and in three hours it would be dawn.

"I think Mum will be a bit better, now," he said. "May, do you think I could have a couple of aspirins, and lie down? I've got such a splitting headache."

"Of course, Mick," May said and squeezed his hand. "You've been wonderful."

"*You* have, you mean."

They passed each other, and May went up to Mrs. Bryant's room. She was sitting on the side of the bed, looking at a photograph of herself and her husband, which had been taken a year before. She didn't turn her head when May came in. It was ten minutes before May could persuade her to take the tablets, drink the milk and lie down. She lay on her back, staring at the ceiling, her belt and skirt loose, and her shoes off.

Now, the house was silent.

Micky slept in a tiny cubicle which his father had partitioned off from the room where the younger boys slept; it gave him a little privacy. May saw the light go out under his door. She closed her eyes as she went downstairs, feeling dizzy and sick with tiredness and fear for Derek; now that there was no one to help, it was much more difficult to keep going. She went into the kitchen. There was a couch which she had slept on occasionally, in emergency; she would again to-night. She felt cold, and very lonely. It was as if ghosts were walking the house.

She put on her thick overcoat, pulled a blanket over her, and punched two cushions into position. She didn't expect to sleep, just to rest and ease her aching eyes and head. If she felt like this, what on earth did Mum feel like?

She began to doze.

She went to sleep.

One of the children woke her when it was broad daylight. Pam, the girl. May sat bolt upright and clutched her, almost scaring the girl with her intensity.

"Pam, what is it? What's the matter?"

"Mummy's fast asleep," Pam said, "and Daddy still isn't there. And I'm afraid I'll be late for school."

"For school," echoed May. "Yes, what a fool I am!" She pushed the blanket back and got up. "Pam, put a kettle on, there's a dear, and then go and get washed and dressed. Are the others awake yet?"

"Bob is too, but Tim isn't."

Tim was the three-year-old.

"Don't wake Tim then, but tell Bob to get washed and dressed. If you're late for school I'll come and tell the teacher that it was my fault."

Pam went into the scullery; happier.

Still hardly awake, May pulled up the spring blind of the kitchen so that more light came in. The window overlooked a brick wall which divided this garden from the one next door; and, beyond the wall, the window of the next house. It was drab and gray, but the morning was bright, and frost sparkled on some slates.

Pam was filling the kettle.

"I couldn't even wake Mummy," she announced.

"Couldn't *wake* her," May echoed.

In sudden panic, she went quickly to the stairs and hurried up. She could hear the younger children talking; so Tim was awake. She hesitated outside Mrs. Bryant's door, her heart thumping. Was it only the sleeping draught?

She opened the door.

The room was nearly in darkness; light came from the sides of the windows, that was all. She hurried and released the blind, then stopped it from banging. She turned and went toward Kath Bryant, hands outstretched.

It was all right; thank God, it was all right. The older woman was asleep; May could see movement at her breast and lips. It was just the effect of the sleeping tablets, then. That silly fear—it wasn't much after nine, she'd hardly been asleep for three hours!

May tiptoed out.

She listened at the door of the room which Derek and Micky shared. There was no sound. She felt her heart pounding, opened the door, and peeped in.

Derek's bed was empty; so he wasn't back.

May went downstairs, heavy-hearted, made tea, and then heard a knock at the front door. Mingled hope and fear flared up. She saw herself in the mirror, but hardly noticed that she had on no make-up, that her short fair hair was untidy, her thick, green coat was creased and crumpled.

It was Mrs. Rosa Trentham, from across the road, Mrs. Bryant's oldest and one close friend. She'd been out on the night of the news, but had spent most of yesterday here. Behind her were several other neighbors; behind them, a dozen strangers including several men; and there was a policeman in uniform, looking very official. It had been like this most of yesterday.

"Let me in and then close the door, May," Rosa Trentham said. "I've come to help."

She cooked breakfast and got the children

ready; another neighbor took them to school . A third carried off three-year-old Tim, as she had yesterday. Mrs. Bryant was to sleep in as long as she could, and May *must* rest. As soon as either of them was awake, they must send for the neighbor next door, across the road, anywhere.

Let Kath Bryant sleep.

Let Micky sleep.

And May must get some sleep herself—why not use the girls' room?

It sounded heavenly. If only Derek—

May went to bed, secure with Rosa Trentham's promise to call her if any word came from Derek.

When she did wake, everything was different. There was no sense of shock or surprise, and she lay for a few minutes, comfortably warm except for her right shoulder. She shrugged the clothes over it and lay on her back. Then, like a heavy blow, came realization that there could have been no word from Derek.

The sickening anxiety came back.

She glanced at the old-fashioned alarm clock on the mantelpiece; it said five minutes to two. Slowly, she sat up. It was colder than she had realized, and she flung the bedclothes back and grabbed the green coat, which would serve as a dressing gown; the lining stuck cold on her bare arms and shoulders.

Someone was moving about up here.

It might be Mum Bryant or one of the neighbors; or, she supposed, the police.

She opened her door and went onto the landing.

Mrs. Bryant's door was closed. May turned the handle cautiously, and opened it a shade. The blinds were still drawn. She fancied that she heard the sound of even breathing; certainly she didn't hear a whisper. She closed the door as softly as she had opened it, and then turned toward the head of the stairs. She heard something squeak, followed by a muttered exclamation, and fancied that it was a man's voice.

The police? Who else could it be?

May supposed Rosa Trentham's husband might have come.

Derek?

She hurried downstairs, quite wide awake; it did not even occur to her that there might be anything to fear.

The movements were in the room immediately below the main bedroom—a tiny middle room used for all kinds of purposes. Ironing, packing, storing, and "office." Tom Bryant had done a great deal of voluntary work, for the chapel and for two of his clubs, and he always used a small roll-top desk in that room.

The door was ajar.

Who would be in that room?

The police probably felt that they had to search everywhere, but—

May opened the door wide.

A man was standing at the desk, and turning round toward the door. He wore a scarf over his face, and a peaked cap pulled low over his forehead; it was like a scene out of a film.

In his right hand he held a big iron bar.

May stood with her hands raised and her mouth wide open, but she didn't scream; she couldn't make a sound. Something told her that the man was as scared as she. It was impossible to be sure how long they stayed like that, how long it was before she managed to gasp:

"What are you doing here?"

As she spoke, she swung round, to run. The man leaped at her. She began to scream, but before a sound came out, his hand clapped over her mouth. She felt the pressure first of his hand, then of his body against her. She could see the iron bar, in her mind's eye, and remembered vividly what had happened to Tom Bryant. She kicked and struck out, and plucked at the scarf, but it was useless; she couldn't push the man away. She felt herself being pressed tighter against the wall, and a hand tightened round her throat. Then she felt something drop on her right foot, and the next moment the other hand closed round her throat, throttling her. She writhed and tried to scream and kicked out helplessly; the felt slippers made no impression, and she couldn't breathe.

Her lungs seemed to be getting fuller, with a band round them, gripping as tightly as the fingers gripped her throat. She felt her strength ebbing.

She could hear herself pleading:

"Don't kill me, please don't kill me. Please don't kill me!" She hardly knew the measure of her own despair, or the certainty that death was coming. There were shimmery figures in front of her eyes; bright lights, white and yellow and flashes of red. Red, yellow, white. Dots and dashes. There was worse pain at her throat and at her lungs, and she felt the strength oozing out of her legs and arms. She knew that her arms hung limp by her sides now, and felt her legs sagging. She was just conscious of the fact that only the man's grip on her throat was holding her up.

In hopeless, helpless horror, she was still pleading to him with her own inward voice, the voice which only she could hear.

"Please don't kill me, please don't kill me."

She was losing consciousness.

"Oh, God, don't let him kill me, don't let me die."

The light vanished, and there was only blackness, until she ceased to be aware of pain.

The man drew back.

He was gasping for breath, and sweat beaded his forehead and his upper lip. His mouth was open, and his teeth showed. He looked down at the heap that was May Harrison. She had fallen on her left side, and her face was turned away from him, but he could see the slackness at her lips, and the puffiness at her throat. The coat gaped open. She wore a white slip underneath, of some shimmery kind of stuff, and some frilly lace at the top and the bottom. She didn't move, didn't seem to breathe.

He gulped.

Slowly, he went toward the door and listened intently, but he heard no sound.

He picked up the iron bar.

It was just a crowbar; a jimmy. He weighted it in his right hand, while he looked down on the girl. His breath was rasping between his lips now.

"She didn't—she *couldn't* have seen me," he muttered.

His hand went to his face. The scarf was down about his neck and if anyone saw him now they would see him clearly. He didn't know whether the girl had seen him properly or not.

"She couldn't have," he said aloud, and then after a pause: *"Could she?"*

He went down on one knee, felt for her hand, then for her wrist. He couldn't feel the pulse beating; he didn't think he could, anyhow, but his own heart was racing so fast that he couldn't be sure. Her arm was limp enough; she *looked* dead.

He glanced at the jimmy.

He raised it.

He shuddered, and then thrust the jimmy in between his shirt and his trousers, and turned to Tom Bryant's desk. He had searched everything except two drawers, and now started to look again, with feverish haste. Every few seconds he glanced round at May, and she didn't move.

If she was dead, he was a killer.

She couldn't have seen his face, could she?

He finished searching, and felt sure that he wouldn't find what he had come for; what he had been sent for. He shivered again. He had two fears: that he might be trapped here, and that the girl might have caught a glimpse of his face before he had closed with her.

She couldn't have.

Anyhow, she was dead.

And if she wasn't dead, she damned soon would be.

He eased his collar, touched the handle of the jimmy again, and began to draw it from his waistband. Then as he did so, he heard a sound. It was as if an electric current had been switched on inside him; fear came in a single, searing flash.

A key was in the lock. He could hear it turning. He heard a man say: "Well, no one's come out."

"You're not coming *in,"* a woman said brusquely.

"You newspaper people ought to be ashamed of yourselves, pestering the lives out of someone who's had such a terrible loss."

"Now be a friend," the man began. "Let's have a word or two from you, Mrs. Trentham, and we won't worry you anymore."

The door slammed.

The woman who had let herself in with the key came walking briskly from the front door; and she would have to pass this door, which was ajar. She would be within a foot or two of the crouching man and the girl who lay so still.

Now, the jimmy was held tightly in the man's right hand.

9

May

Mrs. Rosa Trentham, friend and neighbor of the Bryants for twenty years, closed the front door on the newspaper reporter and then walked quickly and angrily toward the kitchen. As she neared the foot of the stars and the little room close by, she bit her lips in vexation. The slamming door might wake Kath, May, or Micky. She stopped just outside the door of the little room, listening for any indication that any of the three were awake. It was after two, and she consoled herself that it wouldn't be too serious if they did wake up; they'd had a good rest.

There was the problem of Kath Bryant, and how best to help her.

Rosa Trentham heard no sound from upstairs, and began to smile and to relax. She actually took a step toward the kitchen door, which was wide open, when she saw the door of the little room move slightly; then a sound came, a sharp hissing noise which scared her.

"What—" she began.

The door was pulled open. She saw a man with a scarf over his face, his left hand level with the handle of the door and his right hand raised and holding an iron bar.

She screamed.

She turned and rushed toward the front door, shouting, "*Help, help!*" The man struck at her once, and she felt a blow on her shoulder, but it didn't stop her. "*Help, help!*" she screeched and touched the catch of the door with her outstretched hand. "*Help, murder!*"

For all she knew, a second, murderous blow would fall. She couldn't shout again, but pulled at the catch desperately. For the next few seconds she knew only terror; but the man didn't strike again.

He was at the back of the house, climbing out of the kitchen window, preparing to race toward the service alley, his motorcycle, and another street.

Cyril Dawson, of the *Globe*, had almost given up his vigil at the Bryants' house, and that was not simply because he was out of patience. He didn't think he would get anywhere if he stayed all day. He knew that neighbors went in and out every hour or so, and so waited for the next visit. It was Mrs. Trentham, and she was a few minutes late. He wasn't surprised at her response to his plea, and in fact was amused by her pretended indignation. He shrugged and turned away, smiling knowingly at the middle-aged policeman who was near the edge of the pavement. A dozen people, mostly women, were standing around to catch a glimpse of the family whose pictures and names were in the papers.

"I'll call it a day," Dawson said.

"Can't understand why they pay you to hang around like this," the policeman said.

"Who said they pay me?" Dawson asked, and turned toward the corner.

As he did so, he heard a scream.

He swung round toward the little crowd; the women suddenly went tense, and all listlessness vanished. The policeman winced, as if he'd been hurt, then launched himself forward. He snatched and blew his whistle, and the blast echoed up and down the street.

He flung himself at the door.

"Help, help!" the scream kept coming. "Murder! Help!"

The constable swung from the door toward the window, and cracked the glass with his truncheon. Ignoring the splinters, he put his head down and plowed a way through, his helmet pushing the longest splinters aside.

As the noise died down, a car turned into the street, and another policeman came running from the corner.

The door opened.

Rosa Trentham came stumbling out, mouth wide open and hands raised, gray hair pulled out of its neat bun and straggling round her neck, her face distorted. Dawson was just in front of her, and she fell into his arms. He could hear her sobbing breath and feel the shuddering tension of her body. From the doorway, he saw nothing but the open door of the kitchen and the stairs leading upward, but the policeman appeared from a room at one side, truncheon in hand, massive and swift moving. He turned and raced toward the kitchen door.

"What was it?" Dawson asked shrilly. "What was it?"

Mrs. Trentham just gasped and sobbed.

Dawson eased the woman aside and, as others came up, said hastily: "Look after her," and ran into the house.

Three things seemed to happen at once. There was another blast of a police whistle, a long way off. There was a black-haired youth in battle dress standing at the head of the stairs, looking scared and unsteady; and there was the open door of the little room, and a girl's hair.

The Harrison girl's.

"My God!" breathed Dawson. He thrust the door wider open and stepped inside, and saw May Harrison. He took one look, then put his head round the door and shouted: "Send for a doctor! Get a move on, send for a doctor!" He went back to the girl, who was lying in an odd position on the floor, and now he was torn between helping her and rushing to a telephone.

Her neck was red and puffy. There were scratches at her cheeks. He felt her pulse, holding his breath as he did so. It was beating, but was very, *very* faint. She needed artificial respiration, *now.*

"What about that doctor?" he shouted.

Two women had come in from the street, with another policeman. The boy in battle dress was saying urgently: "He says we ought to get a doctor, please hurry." One of the women said brusquely:

"Now don't take on, Micky, I'm as good as any doctor, any day." It was one of the neighbors, and what she said wasn't even remotely true, but it steadied Micky. Then, the policeman started to take command, telling them what to do, and began artificial respiration expertly. That took the responsibility from Dawson, and within three minutes he was at a telephone. The *Globe* had the story before the Yard, but within a few minutes of its reaching the Yard, Turnbull was told.

And he told Roger.

Roger saw Dawson of the *Globe*, the man who had been at the Mansion House, among the crowd now fifty or sixty strong which had gathered outside the Bryants' house. There was a tall policeman, too, who didn't recognize Roger and who stood at the open doorway as if he meant to make sure that no one passed.

Dawson would tell the story best.

"How long have you been here?" Roger asked.

"Three hours," said Dawson promptly. He had a boyish face and wispy hair which was so fair that the gray in it wasn't noticed. He told what he knew, and added that he had telephoned the *Globe*, and just come back to pick up the rest of the story. "I think I've earned my special interview," he added, and grinned.

"How's Miss Harrison?"

"The doctor's with her now," Dawson said, and his grin vanished. "If you ask me—"

"Not dead, is she?"

"No, I shouldn't think so."

Roger felt the knifelike stab at his heart; the fear above all fears that a murder which should have been prevented had been committed. If that girl— well, she wasn't dead yet, was she? He forced himself to speak sarcastically.

"So you've made a hero of yourself for the sake of an exclusive interview?"

"If you want a hero, take the copper," Dawson said. "I've never seen a chap take a header into a glass window before. He doesn't know it, but he'll be on the front page of the *Globe* in the morning, and if you could add a caption—"

"Make your own; it'll be much better," Roger said. "But if I can fix you something later, I will. Don't crowd me or the Bryant family, though."

"Handsome," said Dawson, "I was in the house, I was the first to find the girl, I was with the brother who didn't know whether he was coming or going, and I didn't ask him a single question, just calmed him down. There's restraint for you."

Roger said:"Thanks. I hope your editor doesn't sack you."

He moved toward the open front door, where Kilby was standing with the constable on guard; a constable now eager to please. Kilby looked big and burly and tense; he wasn't a tense man by nature.

"Hallo," Roger said to the constable. "Crowd's not being too much of a nuisance, I hope."

"Oh, no, sir."

"Good."

Young Micky was standing on the second or third stair and looking into the room where May Harrison lay. An ambulance bell rang outside. Roger went nearer to the door. A woman he didn't recognize was bending over the girl, and applying artificial respiration. Another stood with her arm round Mrs. Bryant. A doctor was standing up, a little man, elderly, harassed looking.

Kilby muttered: "If that girl's dead—"

"Shut up."

"Sorry."

Kath Bryant was looking at the doctor, as if she was looking at the judgment seat. Her heart, her very life, was in her eyes. Her hands were held forward in silent supplication. It lasted only for a few seconds, yet the silence and the poignancy would be hard to forget.

The doctor said: "She's coming round. I'm going to get her to the hospital as soon as I can, and make sure she's all right. Didn't I hear the ambulance bell?"

There was a bustle at the doorway. Kilby should have been making sure that the ambulance men could come straight in, but instead he was peering over the heads of the women, looking toward May Harrison. Her lips were moving now, and she was gasping for breath. Roger beckoned the men, and pushed Kilby aside. May's face looked swollen, and her neck was very red and angry looking. The blood which had welled up from the scratches was vivid.

"See them out when the doctor gives the word," Roger said to Kilby.

"Eh? Oh, yes. See them out." Kilby threw off his preoccupation, and went to the door to make sure that there was no crushing. More people had come along at the sound of the ambulance bell. Kilby bellowed at them, as if to relieve his feelings.

Soon, the doctor gave the word to move the girl.

The ambulance men were quick and gentle. As they lifted May on the stretcher, Roger watched Kath Bryant in her agony. Young Micky Bryant was still on the stairs, and when May was taken out, he said in a strangled voice:

"She—she isn't dead?"

"No, she isn't," Roger said, deliberately sharp. "Don't make things out to be worse than they are. Do you know what happened?"

"No. I—I heard someone screaming, came rushing down and—and there was May on the floor, and—"

Micky broke off; voice quivering.

Roger offered him a cigarette, and he took it eagerly.

"If I were you," said Roger, "I'd go and put a kettle on . If I know women, your mother and her friends will want a cup of tea. Get some aspirins, too." He spoke as he went into the kitchen. He could see that the back door was open, and saw a constable approaching, probably the man who had chased the girl's assailant.

The constable was walking slowly, and breathing very hard. He hadn't a scratch, but a sliver of glass, six inches long, was sticking out of his helmet. Obviously he didn't realize that. Two other policemen were in the service alley at the end of the little garden, and Roger could hear them talking.

"No luck?" said Roger. "I hear you had a good try."

The constable said: "Who are—" and then backed a pace. "Sorry, Mr. West, didn't recognize you. No, no luck, sir. The swine turned right out of the gate, and had a motorbike waiting. He didn't take long scorching along that alley. I caught a glimpse of his back, that's all. I've already telephoned a message to the Division, sir, I'm sure they'll send a squad along. My colleagues are searching the lane to see whether the chap dropped anything, or whether there are any footprints or tire tracks. Not likely to be many, I'm afraid; it's a tarred path."

"Never know your luck," said Roger. "Any idea what he was after?"

"Afraid I haven't, sir."

"We'd better go and see if we can find out," Roger said.

If there was anything he didn't want to do, it was increase the pressure on Mrs. Bryant; but it had to be done.

She looked dreadful when he spoke to her.

"Mrs. Bryant," he said, "do you know why anyone should come and attack May? Any reason why anyone would want to break into the house?"

"No," Mrs. Bryant said flatly.

"Did your husband confide in you about everything?"

"Yes, everything."

"Do you know what he was doing with a hundred pound note in his pocket when he was killed?" Roger asked, abruptly.

She looked astounded; and it was easy to believe her when she gasped: "Tom with a hundred pounds? Nonsense! It—it just can't be true."

He assured her that it was, but doubted whether he had convinced her. That hundred pounds made a mystery of its own, and possibly held the key to the problem. He would have to worry it.

Roger saw the desk in the little room, obviously ransacked, and looked through it; there was nothing of interest, but at least it was obvious that the motorcyclist had come to search the house, and had made a beeline for dead Bryant's desk.

Why?

As far as Roger could judge, Mrs. Bryant really

didn't know, and a detailed search of the room revealed nothing. He left a man to go through the rest of the house, and went back to the Yard. Traffic was thick on the Embankment, and the journey took nearly half an hour.

On his desk was a note in the Assistant Commissioner's thick, heavy writing.

"Call me at once."

Well, Chatworth would have to wait for a few minutes. Roger put in a call to the hospital where May Harrison had been taken. Once he established himself as a Yard man, he was put through to the Ward Sister at once, but she had to go and make inquiries. Roger tapped the desk impatiently with his pencil.

The door opened and Chatworth came in. He was a Goliath of a man who seemed to push the door back with his paunch, and stride forward. The door swung to behind him. He glowered across at Roger, who raised a hand, but kept the telephone to his ear. Chatworth came over, walking heavily, and Roger put a hand over the mouthpiece and said:

"Won't you sit down, sir."

"Hallo, Chief Inspector," the Sister said. "I'm afraid I've no further news for you. Miss Harrison is conscious but suffering severely from shock. Can I telephone you if there is any further news?"

Roger said: "I'll be grateful if you will. And will you give a message to Detective Sergeant Kilby, who's at the hospital?"

"Gladly."

"Ask him to stand by until I send a policewoman," said Roger. "And I'll be grateful if you'll

91

allow the policewoman to sit by Miss Harrison's bed."

"Very well," the Sister said.

Roger thanked her, rang off, and put the receiver down. He didn't speak at once. Chatworth still wasn't pleased, but no longer looked so annoyed.

"Now, what's it all about?" he asked. "I thought everything was over bar the shouting when we got this Wilson chap and the prints. What on earth did a thief want in the Bryants' house?"

"All we know is that he searched the room where Bryant used to do his spare-time work," Roger said. "So far we haven't found a single print there or a scrap of evidence—except that he wore a brown suit and a cap. No one seems to have seen the motorcycle clearly enough to tell us what make it was."

"Better use the B.B.C. again," Chatworth suggested.

"I'd like to do that," Roger said, and tried to throw off the depression which had settled when he had seen May Harrison on the floor. At least Chatworth was not being bloody-minded. "What about the wholesale fingerprinting at River Way?"

"The P.M.G. says he'll storm the Home Secretary's office to stop it—these Post Office chaps are just about as keyed-up as they can be," Chatworth said morosely. "Only sense I got out of him was that two days before Christmas the rush should have steadied. I know we don't want to wait, but we can't do that job without full Home Office approval, and it might have to go to the Cabinet. Can you wait?"

"Looks as if we'll have to," Roger said. "Can't

expect everyone to see it our way." He lit a ciga-rette, as Chatworth took a packet of cheroots from his pocket. "The case won't open out," he com-plained. "We're as far off a motive as ever. Young Derek Bryant's been gone for two days without a trace. Now this attack. If Tom Bryant had been a big-time crook, the pace couldn't be hotter."

"Think he was?"

"Dr. Jekyll and Mr. Hyde? The truth is, I can't even begin to guess. I'd give a lot to find Derek Bryant."

"Who has a motorcycle," Chatworth put in.

Roger said irritably: "Oh, I've considered the possibility that Derek killed his father, went into hiding, and was driven back home to get some-thing, but it's still guesswork."

"Anything from this woman of Carmichael's, the Chief Sorter?"

"Not yet. Turnbull's having them both watched. The woman has a flat in a house at St. John's Wood, and there's no doubt Carmichael pays the rent. No law against it."

"Has Carmichael any private means?"

"We haven't traced any. He lives by himself in a little house at Paddington, humble as can be."

"What about this man Simm and the van rob-bery?" asked Chatworth.

"He's been in the service for twenty years with-out a blemish," Roger told him, "and there's no doubt the stolen bags could have been taken while the van was at the Post Office. More likely he went to have a drink and won't admit it. Oh, he could be involved, I suppose." Roger was fumbling among the papers on his desk, and picked up an enlarged photograph of a fingerprint. He frowned at it.

"That's all we found to help." He searched again and picked up other, similar photographs. "Print on hammer, and print on the glass at Wilson's room," he said, and added very thoughtfully, "Not a full print among them—each is a fragment." He almost forgot Chatworth's presence as he took a magnifying glass from his desk. There was a full minute's silence. Then: "That's damned odd," he said, "the same section in each case, tented arch, almost identical lines."

"What's so surprising?" Chatworth asked.

"Three fragmentary prints, all identical, means he wears gloves with a hole in one finger or thumb, or has some peculiarity—I'll check with Wilberforce as soon as I can."

Chatworth nodded, and asked: "Anything else at the Sorting Office?"

Roger said very slowly: "No one says much about Derek Bryant, but he wasn't as popular as his father. Farnley the Postmaster is worried about the Christmas mails, but seems anxious to be helpful. Carmichael is very nearly obstructive. Getting the parcels and letters through seems to be an obsession with him, and he's a genius at it. Turnbull's spending all his time on the job and has a couple of good men working with him, but we draw blanks everywhere. Blank on Derek Bryant, blank on Wilson's motor bicycle, blank on motive—"

Roger broke off.

Chatworth drew deeply at a small, black cheroot, put his head on one side, no mean feat for a man with a neck as fat as a bull's, and asked gruffly: "What's got under your skin?"

"I suppose the way the Bryant family has been knocked has really done the damage," Roger said.

"I can't get the wife's face out of my mind. Or May Harrison's. She'll live in hell if Derek did attack her, and she recognized him. From what I can gather she's deeply in love with him, and—" Roger broke off with a wry grin. "You see how dispassionate I am about it all. And I'm reduced to guesswork: that Bryant discovered something at the office, was killed because of it, and the killer has some reason to think he might have kept incriminating evidence which might still be at Clapp Street. And from there," Roger went on heavily, "we have to ask why Bryant sat on something which might be deadly to a killer. Was he the nice chap everyone believed? If there's anything I'd like to be sure of, it's that Tom Bryant is proved to have been in the clear. If we have to smear him, I don't know what will happen to that woman and her family. And if Derek's in it, too—"

"What you want is an early night and an evening with Janet," Chatworth said gruffly. "And as from tomorrow, drop every other job you've got on hand and concentrate on this one. The press is hounding us, the Home Secretary is hounding me, and you're hounding yourself. Give the job all you've got, Roger."

Roger said: "I will. Thanks."

"Anything at the back of your mind?"

"Only the obvious," Roger said. "We've had Post Office van robberies on and off for years. There's always been a certainty that the hold-up men get inside information. Did Bryant stumble on something? Was he first bribed—and then killed to stop him talking? Is there a big haul planned at the River Way Office this Christmas?" He paused, shrugging. Then: "By the way, will you get the

Postmaster General to authorize Farnley, the Postmaster at River Way, to tell me all about the valuables they usually handle? When we know exactly what stuff goes through River Way we might get a line."

"I'll fix it," Chatworth promised.

10

Night

Roger finished a full report at half past six, and slid it into his pocket to read through when he got home. Nothing had come in, but at leasthe had a free hand. He stood up, and went to the door. He wanted to get home, and have an hour with the boys before they went to bed. With luck he would be in time for supper; he would tell the duty sergeant in the main hall to telephone Janet.

As he put a hand on the door, it opened and banged against his foot.

"Sorry," a man said.

Roger pulled the door wider, and saw Kilby moving away. Kilby looked tired; as if he was paying for his late nights. He was a long way from his usual hearty self.

"Ivy Gissing's over at the hospital," he said. "I came straight back."

"How's Miss Harrison?" Roger asked.

Kilby said: "She hasn't said a word. Amnesia following shock is on the records, but she could be

97

foxing." He scowled, savagely. "If she recognized the swine—"

"So you're on the Derek Bryant line too," Roger said. "Come across to the pub and have a drink, and then get home. I'm through for the night."

They were halfway down the outside steps when Roger remembered the message for Janet, and called out to the duty sergeant.

They stepped into Cannon Row, then into a pub; a dozen other Yard men were there; it was hot and smoky and noisy. Roger ordered double whiskies, drank half his, then went to telephone the Inspector in the "back room" who covered the press. When he got back to the bar, he found another double waiting for him; and Kilby's first drink was finished. He didn't say anything, but hoped that Kilby wouldn't start pushing the stuff down too fast.

"Now I'm off," Roger said. "And you get home, too. That's an order."

Kilby said: "Sure."

Roger went back to the Yard for his car. He tried to think of anything that he'd forgotten, and nothing occurred to him. It was nearly half past seven. He drove slowly, as he always did after having a drink, and whenever he had a lot on his mind. Then he decided to drive on to Fulham, and see Mrs. Bryant.

He was with her for only a few minutes, glad that she was surrounded by neighbors.

When he reached Bell Street, no front lights were on at his house. He put the car into the garage, wondering what mood Janet would be in; too often, a bad start in the morning lasted all day, unless he was able to slip indoors for a few minutes; and there just hadn't been a chance. He turned round toward the house, and, as he did so, caught sight of a shadowy figure between him and the back garden; a narrow path led round the side of the house toward it.

He stood quite still, his heart jumping.

Now, there were just the shadows.

Then, there was a giggle.

He felt the tension oozing out of him on the instant, was amazed that he had been so jumpy. He didn't speak as he heard Scoopy, the elder boy, say disgustedly: "Oh, you ass, you're always hopeless. Fancy giggling. Always giggling, that's what you're doing; it's disgusting." Scoopy walked out of the path into the dim light of the street, tall and strong for his eleven years, five feet five inches high and wearing shoes the same size as Roger. "Sorry, Dad," he said, "it was only a joke, but Richard's *hopeless*."

"I don't giggle. And when I do it's because you make faces at me." A smaller figure came out of the darkness, small face set and big eyes flashing. "I wasn't giggling then; I was stopping a sneeze."

"Liar."

"I'm not a liar. Oo, Dad, I'm not a liar. He shouldn't call me a liar when I'm not, should he? I nearly sneezed, and anyhow it's a silly game jumping out at anyone in the darkness. I hate it."

"That's just because you're a miserable little tich," sneered Scoopy.

This could be it; a sharp reproof for both of them, a touchy atmosphere, and the evening probably miserable. The boys didn't behave like this more than once a month, and usually Roger could rely on them to rush at him with the delight they had known since their toddler days.

"Oo, you beast!" Richard's voice was shrill.

Roger gulped.

"Fish," he said, using a diminutive which was confined strictly to the family, "why don't you punch the champ on the nose?"

He stopped.

"Punch—" began Richard, and then giggled. "Well, you hold him, then!"

Scoopy's voice and manner changed completely as he swung round on his father.

"Dad, thanks a lot for calling me champ; isn't it good? I thought it was going to be easy, too, the other chap wasn't so tall as me, but did he pack a punch! Wow! If Mum had been there, I think she would have screamed, and my nose bled a bit, but it wasn't much. You ought to see his right eye; it's closed up and it looks—"

"Just like a ripe tomato," Richard cried. "Scoop didn't half dot him one."

"How I wish I'd been there!" Roger said, and meant it. "Well done, Scoop. Next time I'll make it or bust. How's your mother?"

"Oh, *Mum*," said Scoopy, in a tone which mingled scorn with affection and amusement with both. "She's been impossible all evening, singing those silly songs. You know, calling me a bingbang-bong and—"

"A winky-wong," chimed in Richard.

Roger's heart leaped.

"Let's go and see what she has to say for herself," he said, and, with the boys hanging on to either arm, he went to the front door. Richard took his arm away, and asked swiftly:

"Can I unlock it?"

"Which way do you turn the key?" asked Roger.

"Clock—"

"Fool," breathed Scoopy.

"Counter-clockwise! There, I was right, wasn't I? Clockwise to close it I was going to say, and counter-clockwise to open it."

Roger surrendered the key. Richard turned it this way and that before it opened, then went rushing in, forgetting all about standing aside for his father, calling: "Mum, Dad's home and he's put the car away so he's not going out again. Mum!"

Scoopy shook his head and spoke as if he was talking of his grandson.

"That *child*. I shouldn't think he'd ever grow up; he's even left the key in the lock."

Roger chuckled.

The kitchen door was now wide open, and Janet came from the scullery. The table was laid for Roger alone, but he wasn't worried about the table. He looked into Janet's eyes. They were quite clear of vexation, and had the glow he wanted to see. He put his arms round her and gave her a squeeze and a kiss that left her breathless and then stood back to look at her.

"Hallo, sweet. Anything for a hungry man?"

"It's in the oven. Hot pot. Are you going to have a drink first?"

"I've had one."

"All right," Janet said. "Scoopy, get your father's dinner out of the oven, and be careful, there's a lot of gravy. Don't forget to use the oven cloth; the plate will be hot. Richard, you go and pick up that newspaper and fold it properly, and don't let me have to tell you again."

101

"No, Mum."

"Little beggar," Roger said. He sat down, smiling at Janet. "What kind of a day?"

"Oh, nothing would go right at first," Janet told him. "Then I went out this afternoon and they were talking about that postman's murder. One of the women knows Mrs. Bryant, and when I heard what was happening to her I felt I ought to be kicked. How—how is she?"

Roger said: "In some ways worse." He explained a little about May Harrison, while the boys stood listening intently. He talked more freely an hour later, when the boys were in bed and he sat in the kitchen with a weak whisky and soda by his side, watching Janet making the mincemeat. The easy rhythm of her movements, the sight of her smooth, rounded forearm as she wielded knife and spoon, the smell of the dried fruit and the spices, all had a soothing effect.

"I'll just clear these things away," she said about eleven o'clock. "Mrs. Day will be in in the morning, she can—"

"We'll wash up," Roger said. "It won't take five minutes." He smoked as he dried the dishes, the knives and forks. It was not only good to be home, it was the one place to be. And Janet looked much less tired than she had the previous night; her eyes were brighter, her movements less sluggish.

"Would you like to put the electric fire on in the front room, and have the easy chair for a bit?" she asked.

Roger grinned.

"No," he said.

"It's more comfortable for us both."

"*No*," he insisted, and was still grinning.

102

"But, darling, why—" she began, and then broke off. "Oh, you fool!"

"Fool or not," Roger said, "I know my rights."

The street was very quiet.

Janet lay sleeping, on her left side, and with her back toward Roger. Their legs were touching, but at the shoulders there was a wide gap between them. Roger felt a cold streak down his back, and shifted the bedclothes a little, to try to get rid of it; he failed. It was much colder than it had been, and he could see the frostiness of the stars. He wondered what the weather forecast had been and, idly, whether they would get a white Christmas at last. *I'm dreaming of a white Christmas* . . . Where had he heard that recently? Young voices—oh, damn. Yes.

Janet made funny little puffing noises.

Roger was suddenly wide awake, the glorious afterglow of drowsiness all gone; and he knew that it would be some time before he dropped off. If he got up, he would probably disturb Janet, so he decided to stay there.

He found himself wondering whether Derek Bryant was alive or dead.

May Harrison dozed on and off during the night, aware of a great weariness, of a little pain and of a vagueness. She knew that she was alive, she knew that she lay in a bed, but that was all. Everything else was misty; everything else was forgotten.

Kath Bryant was more wide awake than she had been for a long time; much more alert than she wanted to be. She knew that Rosa or any one of several neighbors would have spent the night with

103

her, but preferred to be on her own, in this room. One half of her mind warned her that in spite of the shock of what had happened, she hadn't fully accepted the truth, yet: she didn't really believe that Tom was dead. There was his place and his pillow; there were his slippers; there was the small Bible, with the tiny print, and with a piece of dry holly as a bookmark, showing what verses he had last read. How many times had he read the Bible through? Several, she believed; and she could also believe that he had known every verse of it by heart.

The younger children were all in their proper beds; asleep.

She was looking through an old cardboard box with old letters and souvenirs: of days' outings with this club or that, with the chapel, with some of the men at the Sorting Office. There were photographs; with Tom at Brighton, with Tom at Southend, with Tom, with Tom, with Tom. And with the children. As she looked at these pictures, quite dry-eyed, she went over what she had told them. She believed that she had been right to be simple and truthful and direct.

Pam had cried and Bob had sniffed. Little Tim had done most harm, with his bright eyes and curly lashes and his piping: "Daddy gone dead?"

Well, they knew and wouldn't have to be told again. She was glad that she had them in the house with her. She was facing it alone, as she would have to in the future.

Derek—where *was* Derek? She hated herself for the things that came to her mind.

And May.

Kath felt choky.

Well, there were the good things. The neighbors.

The police—there was one at the front door and one at the back, now, and that would go on until they were sure that they had the murderer.

There was that plainclothes man, West. She couldn't remember his rank, and it didn't greatly matter. He'd looked in for ten minutes on his way home, and she remembered with a warm gratitude the way his wife had helped her, on that awful night. He hadn't really asked questions, except the one which everyone wanted answered: why had anyone burgled this house? At most, there would be ten pounds in Tom's cash box; anything over that he put into the Post Office, to take out at Christmas. He had this year. How—how on earth had he come by a *hundred* pounds? It was a fortune; as much as their life's savings.

Then why had that brute come here and attacked May?

Where—where was Derek?

She had been through all the papers in the desk downstairs, and found nothing unusual, nothing to give her any idea of the motive.

Unless Tom had robbed—

No!

Why?

Then, picking up several old letters, the envelopes faded and the ink on the addresses turning brown, something heavy fell out of one. It was bright and shining—a key. All she could see at first was that it looked complicated; a Yale type, although larger than a door key. When she picked it up, it reflected the light and momentarily dazzled her, it was so fresh and new.

Aloud, she said: "What on earth did Tom put

that there for?" And after a moment's silence: "What key can it be?"

She hadn't seen one like it before.

She put it back, but kept staring. Her heart began to beat faster. She picked it up again, and then brushed her hair back from her forehead.

Was this what they had been looking for?

Had Tom hidden it here?

She believed, at heart, that he had.

She put it back, and moved slowly to the bed and sat down; it was the first time she had sat down since she had come into the room. There was the photograph of Tom on the mantelpiece, showing his handsome face and his waving gray hair and the smile which had meant everything to her.

Why had he hidden it?

"Tom," she said, in a husky voice. "what is it? Why did you bring it home?"

He was smiling at her.

"I—I don't understand," she said, in a strangled voice. "I don't understand."

But she began to understand her fears.

She got up, and started to walk about, talking as she did so, not loudly, but quite coherently. She ought to tell the police; that man West. Of course the key was the thing which the thief had wanted, what else could it be? But—why had Tom brought it home? What key was it? It looked like a safe key of some kind; certainly it fitted an important lock.

"Tom," she said aloud, "I just don't understand. You—*you* wouldn't have anything to do with—with anything wrong. Would—oh, of course you wouldn't!" She shouted that out. "I'm hateful even to think of it.

"Tom.

106

"What key is it?
Tom, why did you bring it home?"

In another part of London, in St. John's Wood, where Carmichael's blonde had her flat, one man was talking to another. The speaker was the bigger of the two; the second man was younger and slimmer. He looked scared; he was scared. They had the evening newspapers in the room, with the banner headlines about the murders, and another about the attack on May Harrison. They had discarded the newspapers some time ago, and only the one voice had been heard since the last rustling.

"...if she didn't see your face that's okay, because no one else did. And it says in the *Globe* that she's come round dopey so she can't talk, anyway. You're okay for a while. I'm not blaming you for not croaking her; I'm blaming you because you didn't get that key, see. And I've got to get it. I went to a lot of trouble to get hold of that key, and—but we don't have to waste words. I'll bet the key's at Bryant's place."

"I can't break in there again!"

"No one suggested you should try," the larger man said. "There are more ways of killing a cat than choking it with cream. If you can't get in, we've got to fix someone who can, and we've got to do it in a hurry. How about this kid brother, what's his name?"

"Mick—Micky?" the youth said.

"You ought to know. Well, what about Micky? What about persuading him into having a look for it, eh? You ought to be able to do a little thing like that." He paused, and then suddenly let out a great bellow of laughter. "Why didn't I think of that before, eh? That's a hell of a good joke, that is, before I've finished I'll have those ruddy cops chasing their own tails! That's how good I am at thinking things up."

He laughed again.

The younger man didn't speak; just looked uneasy.

He left the house a little after six. A few lights were on at nearby windows, from early risers. His motorcycle was leaning against the wall of the house, and he wheeled it toward the street before starting the engine. It made a raucous din, which grew worse for a few seconds, then began to fade as he drove off into the dark morning.

Mrs. Bryant was praying. "Oh, God, tell me what to do."

11

Morning

Roger West swung the car into Scotland Yard at half past eight next morning, and brought it to within a few inches of the wall, and only a foot from the next car to it. He got out, slammed the door, and walked briskly toward the steps. A Superintendent who was coming down grinned and said: "Nice judgment this morning."

"I just leave it to the car."

"You don't have to tell me." They stopped in the middle of the steps. "Not much in for you during the night, Handsome. That Bryant chap hasn't been home yet, and we had his mother on the line twice."

"Hm. Thanks."

"Nothing happened at the Bryants' place, nothing new in about the Wilson murder—haven't heard of another glimpse of that man who went went home with him."

"Pity."

"Well, get your teeth into it," said the Superintendent breezily. "We want it all over by Christmas."

Roger said: "I've got a family, too."

He went on. He felt better and in a much brighter mood than last night, and reminded himself as he went to the stairs, ignoring the lift, that he was a copper. His job was just catching criminals, from petty thieves to murderers, and there was no point in trying to carry everybody's burden on his shoulders. He would do everything he could to help the Bryants but must not help them at the expense of the case.

He was still bright when he entered the office, where a man stood with his back to the door, looking out of the window, and didn't hear him come in.

Roger said: "Hallo, Kilby, couldn't you sleep?"

Kilby swung round.

He'd slept. His eyes were clear. He'd had a good clean shave and had rubbed powder into his face afterward. He wasn't a bad-looking chap, in a rather unfinished kind of way. His nose was a bit short and his mouth not really a good shape.

"Oh, I slept," he said; "you've never been more right; I was dog-tired last night."

"Weren't we both?"

"Didn't know you ever got tired," said Kilby dryly. "Just after you'd left the pub last night, Turn—Mr. Turnbull came in for a quick one."

"I've known it happen before."

"We had one together and then he ran me home," Kilby said, "and we had a chat on the way."

"Turnbull's always worth listening to," Roger said.

"You're telling me! I—" Kilby broke off. "He

asked me to pass on one or two things, sir; he's got to go out to Paddington first thing in the morning; something's turned up on that pawnbroker's murder. He's put in a written report, of course, but this elaborates it a bit. Er—he said you'd probably want to have his scalp, but—"

Roger was smiling.

"He'll keep it. Go on."

"He listed the priorities this way," said Kilby, flushing a little. "First, what did the thief want at Bryant's place, and why not dig deep among Bryant's friends at the Post Office and his clubs and the chapel? Turnbull said—"

"That sometimes these sanctimonious Bible-thumping types are worse than anyone."

"Well, he did suggest—"

"We're checking," Roger said. "What else?"

"He'd make Derek Bryant absolute priority."

"And next?"

"As a matter of fact, sir, he suggested that it's a good idea to have a go at Carmichael's blonde." Now, Kilby began to go pink. "We can only watch Carmichael, but the blonde may have a past, and if we could prove it, then she'd probably talk. Might be worth trying."

"Social contact with the blonde, I gather," Roger said dryly, "and you're the man to do it."

Now, Kilby turned deep red.

"I don't see why not."

Roger grinned. "Nor do I! She'll spot you for a copper a mile off, but that won't matter; it might scare her. Have a shot, but be careful—don't go and fall for the blonde."

Kilby said: "There's no need to worry about *that*." He was so harsh-voiced, so grim faced, that

111

Roger was startled into surprise. Kilby looked a little shamefaced. It was odd that big men on the force were so often naïve. This case had gone deeply into Kilby though, and might be the making of him.

"Who's worrying?" Roger said briskly. "Is there a late report on the woman?"

"Yes, Mr. Turnbull did it before he left," Kilby said. "It's being typed out; should have copies soon."

"Make sure I get one quickly, but first go through everything outstanding, and see if we've missed anything, will you?" Roger nodded dismissal and Kilby went off, leaving Roger to the mass of reports, clearing up his work on other jobs, and preparing the main summary on this one.

He had twenty minutes by himself, before other C.I.s came in, when there were the inevitable interruptions and one main subject—the Post Office case. The newspapers were full of speculation. One had listed every Post Office mail van robbery in the last five years and announced the fabulous total loot of nearly a million pounds. Some argued that this was all the work of a centrally directed gang; others that it was the work of a dozen or more different individuals. All had one point of agreement.

Each robbery was due to a leakage of information from the Post Office.

One of the C.I.s said:

"Not hearing much from you, Handsome. Which side do you favor?"

"If this is one gang, we ought to start a chicken farm," Roger said, and stood up and went to the window. There was a heavy, yellowish gray bank of cloud across the river, and it looked as if it was coming up from the south. "Snow before the night's out," he said; "that will make life hell for Mr. Carmichael."

He saw the door open.

Kilby came in with a typewritten report, gave a general "Good morning" and made a beeline for Roger. "Here's the stuff on Deirdre Ames," he said.

"Nice name for a blonde," remarked Roger.

"Have a look at her photograph," Kilby said, and produced one from between the pages of the report.

Deirdre Ames was really something.

This was a studio portrait of the kind that one found outside less reputable night clubs and third-rate music halls. Deirdre Ames had a great big smile and a great big cleft in a bosom only partly concealed by a great big feather fan. As a photograph, it was a work of art. The odd thing was that in spite of the tawdriness of her outfit, and the way her charms were emphasized, she did not look vulgar. Her eyes seemed not only beautiful but intelligent.

Roger put his head on one side as he looked up at Kilby.

"I told you before, you'd better look after your Boy Scout badges; she'll be after them. But that was probably taken ten years ago when she was at her peak."

"On the back, it says January this year," Kilby pointed out. "About six months before she picked up with old Carmichael."

Roger said: "Hmm," and was as thoughtful as he sounded. If the girl was really like this now, what had she seen in the Chief Sorter? What would any

113

young girl see, except money? There was as yet no evidence about the source of Carmichael's income but this was an indication of its size. The attraction certainly wasn't personal magnetism.

Roger scanned the report.

Deirdre Ames had no record. She had been on the stage, mostly in the chorus, since she was sixteen, and she was now twenty-three. In the past twelve months she had been a cabaret star in a respectable hotel, the Mitham, in a street off Piccadilly. She had shared a small flat with another girl, Muriel Paisley, until July of this year, when she had gone to the apartment which Carmichael paid for. Although Carmichael lived in a much humbler place, he spent a lot of time with his lady love; much of it by night.

Kilby began to fidget.

Roger looked up from the report.

"Syd," he said in a quiet voice, "you'll want to kick me, but I don't think you're the man to tackle Deirdre Ames. I don't think it would be a good idea for her to know that a policeman's after her—I think she ought to be tabbed by someone who isn't likely to be suspected. But there's a job you can do, probably better than anyone else."

Kilby's expression of disappointment was momentary; soon he said cheerfully: "Well, you're the boss. What's the other job?"

"You haven't been to the River Way Sorting Office, have you?"

"No."

"And you've only seen Derek Bryant, of the Post Office people," Roger went on, "and that in the dark."

"That's right."

114

"Syd, go along and get into an old suit, then take a job as a temporary postman at River Way. Try to make it an inside job, so that you're on the spot all the time. The way they lug those parcels about suggests they could use someone with a good pair of shoulders; you'll probably be the answer to Carmichael's prayer. We won't pull any strings. Take your Army discharge papers along, and pitch some story about why you're out of work for the time being and want to make a bit for Christmas. Just keep your eyes wide open. Pick up as much as you can about the routine of the job, especially the registered parcels, and see what you can find out about valuable stuff that goes through the office—how easy it is for an outsider to pick that kind of thing up. Got it?"

"I'm on," Kilby said warmly.

"Good. Report by telephone when you can. Carmichael is one of the main men to watch, so is anyone who seems to have a special claim on him—anyone with whom he seems friendly. Get the regular postmen's opinion of Carmichael, too. Pal up with the van driver named Simm. Get as far inside that job as it's possible to get, but don't stick your neck out and show that you're with us. Keep off the murder as much as you can. Offer to work as much overtime as they want, and generally make yourself useful."

"That's me," said Kilby. He gave a quick, rather warming smile, which took away much of that unfinished look. "Any idea who you'll put on to Deirdre Ames?"

"No. Any ideas yourself?"

"Yes," said Kilby. "I was thinking about that

coming up this morning, and told myself that Silver was really the right man for the job."

"Yes," agreed Roger, "you're probably right."

It was commonly believed at the Yard that no C.I.D. man in the history of the Department had ever been like Johnny Silver. If there was a type of confidence trickster, Silver was the type. He looked it, being sleek and always well-turned-out and slightly overhearty. He talked like it, having a ready tongue, a nice brand of flattery and a reasonable wit. He was in the middle forties and looked ten years younger, was never without a smile and —almost unique at the Yard—he had never stepped into the witness box to give evidence for the prosecution. It was doubtful whether a dozen people, outside the Yard itself, knew that Silver held the rank of Detective Inspector, C.I.D. It was practically certain, because of his characteristics and his usefulness in his present job, that he would never get further promotion unless, simply for the payroll and his pension, he became a C.I. If that worried him, he had never let anyone realize it. He was allowed the largest expense sheet in the Criminal Investigation Department, the items were seldom questioned, and it was known that he could put down whisky faster than anyone else at the Yard. No one had ever known him even slightly tipsy. There had been the famous occasion when he had drunk a team of American and Dutch con men under the table, making them miss a plane and thus ensuring that they were kept on English soil long enough for extradition warrants to catch up with them.

He was full of party tricks.

He practiced a little sleight-of-hand, which was always useful, and knew more card tricks than most. Taken by and large, he was the most likable of men. Big-time crooks, like the Dutchman and the American, always seemed to recognize a fellow traveler, and therein lay their downfall.

Roger checked with the Superintendent who used Silver most, made sure that he could be freed for this job, and sent for him. He was in the office a little after ten o'clock, tall, slim, beautifully tailored in navy blue, hair as shiny as a raven's wing and almost as black, a gold ring with a single small diamond on the little finger of his left hand.

"Now what have I done?" he asked.

"You've only just started," Roger said. "Do you know the Mitham Hotel?"

"Leek Street, Piccadilly," answered Silver promptly. "Edwards and Edwards proprietors, Victor Munro, manager, Sybil Munro his wife-housekeeper, Mario the chef, Bill Higgins the headwaiter—good second-class hotel with a floor show and one, repeat one, real hot dish. Name of Deirdre, often called Didi by her friends. The pianist is Bill Rocky, the violinists variable, the cello a woman named Grant. Mammoth. I'll give you ten to one that your interest in on Didi."

"That's it," said Roger. He briefed Silver, quickly, and Silver said thoughtfully: "I think I can do a bit with her, but it won't be until tonight. It might take two or three nights, too. She's got a Daddy somewhere."

"It's her Daddy we're really interested in," Roger said.

Silver hadn't been gone two minutes before a messenger brought a chit from Chatworth. There was still no permission to take all the fingerprints at River Way, but a note from the Postmaster General's office instructed Farnley to give Roger all information he required. Farnley would not like it, but Christmas rush or not, he'd have to tell Roger about all the valuable post packets that went through River Way.

Since the new office had been opened, countless valuables had gone through it. Much of the diamond trade between this country, the United States and the Netherlands passed through—always under guard. Big shipments of used treasury notes were also channeled through the new office, and although these now had a ceiling of ten thousand pounds in any one consignment, to make sure that no loss could be too severe, very large sums went through in the course of a week.

Roger checked the van drivers and the guards.

He went to River Way, about noon, and the stream of traffic coming out of the main gates was so great that he left his car on the river side of the Embankment, and walked quickly toward the office. For the first time he began to understand and sympathize with Carmichael's obsession. It seemed incredible that so many parcels existed. Vanload after vanload was waiting for the chutes, the loading platforms were piled almost ceiling high; where dozens of men had worked yesterday, now there were hundreds. Young girls and middle-aged women were walking out with satchels of letters on their backs. Boys, middle-aged men and ancients were busy. A few brawny men were unloading the parcels from the vans, and Roger saw

118

one man, in a T-shirt and blue jeans, heaving parcels as if he had been used to it all his life.

Kilby.

When Kilby wanted to move, how he moved! And the fact that he had been taken on and put to work so quickly proved two things: Carmichael was desperately short of labor, and there was no real attempt made at screening the temporary workers.

There was Carmichael, too.

Roger felt his reluctant admiration for the man increase. He moved about quite calmly and coolly, almost serene. Where others were flustered, he took it all in his stride. He seemed to be in a dozen places at once; wherever a heap of parcels was too high, wherever a chute seemed blocked, wherever new vans arrived, there he was giving instructions. Sometimes he guided a van as it reversed into a vacant spot on the platform. He would go among the parcels, and every now and again pick one up and put it gently into a wicker basket with big wheels.

Roger went to him.

"Chief Inspector," greeted Carmichael, quietly, "unless it is of vital importance I really can't spare you any time this morning."

"A few questions, while you're here. Have those three registered bags turned up?"

"No."

"Anything else missing?"

"Not as far as I can trace."

"Derek Bryant?"

"Not to my knowledge, but then he is not in my department, he is in maintenance. I—" Carmichael broke off, wrinkling his nose in a disgust which had nothing to do with the questions. "Idiots," he said, and dived into a pile of two or three hundred parcels and picked one up which was stained on the outside—stained a damp, reddish brown. "When *are* people going to learn not to send raw meat through the post unless securely boxed?— there should be a law, there really should be a regulation. I am always asking Mr. Farnley to try to arrange a deputation to the Postmaster General." He picked the parcel up by its string, and placed it disdainfully into the second of the two baskets. "It must have been in the mail for two days or more; can you smell it?"

Roger said ruefully: "Smell is hardly the word."

"If you were to spend the next few days with us you would begin to understand our problems," Carmichael said earnestly. He dived again, and this time picked up a parcel which was so badly battered that a cloth which wrapped up the contents was poking out. "Every day—*every day*—we get hundreds of parcels which cannot be delivered, hundreds that we have to repack. If the public were less spoon-fed they might take more trouble, but I confess I sometimes wonder."

He dropped another parcel into the big basket.

"See that, Chief Inspector? Just addressed to Aunt Sally. If one hadn't a sense of humor—"

Carmichael broke off as a huge van came slowly toward the loading platform, backing into a space which was scarcely large enough for it. He was guiding it in when an elderly postman came up.

"Registers, Mr. Carmichael."

"All right, I'll come," said Carmichael. He moved off almost at once, took a key from his pocket, and unlocked the back of a small red van.

There were five green canvas bags; the registered bags. He signed the van driver's sheet for them, then carried them into the Sorting Office to his own desk. Alongside this sat a younger man surrounded by a mass of papers. "Sign for these, Jim, and then get them open," Carmichael ordered. He glanced at Roger, and there was a faint, almost likable smile on his face. "You see how careful we are! And if there are important loads, we send a guard with the driver, of course, and at times we send a car after the van to make *quite* sure that nothing can go wrong."

He went out.

A boy with corn-colored hair, very blue eyes, and the look of the Scandinavian, was standing at the loading platform. He was holding a parcel which Roger thought he had seen before: the parcel of meat which was decomposing.

"Please, I am to bring this to you," he said, in careful English.

"That's right, thank you," Carmichael said. He took the parcel gingerly, holding it by the string. The Scandinavian lad managed not to wrinkle his nose, but several others nearby caught a whiff, and waxed sarcastic.

That wasn't all.

Among the men who were making such a show was Kilby, but it wasn't quite the same. He kept pointing at the parcel, and made signs with his hands, twisting them about and then suddenly diving a hand into his pocket and taking out a knife.

Roger nodded.

Kilby stopped his pantomime, picked up a sack

of parcels and walked with them toward the chutes.

"You see, another," said Carmichael. "Exactly the same—*No such address in S.W.6. Try adjoining districts.* I really must arrange for these to be taken to the refuse disposal dump at once."

Roger said: "Hold that a minute. Wasn't it the same address as the last one?"

"I really didn't notice," Carmichael said, "and it doesn't really matter. If a man will do a senseless thing once, he will do it again."

Roger was burrowing. The smell was overpowering, now, the kind of smell he didn't like at all; perhaps that was why Kilby wanted the parcel opened. He had often had to endure it, when called to the scene of murder. The odor of decomposing flesh was always much the same.

He found the first parcel, addressed in block lettering, to: *Mr. Smith, 29 Simca Road, S.W.6.* The second parcel had been addressed in the same kind of handwriting, on brown paper which had absorbed some of the ink.

Carmichael was called to another van.

Roger took out his pen knife, and slashed the string of the second parcel. As he did so, a small van backed in. When the doors were opened hundreds of turkeys came in sight hanging by their feet to bars which had been fitted into the top of the van. Each bird was labeled, each plucked, each looked fresh and wholesome.

Any turkey that rubbed shoulders with a parcel like this wouldn't be at home on his Christmas table.

He unwrapped the putrefying flesh.

He winced.

For he was looking at a human arm—cut off at the shoulder and above the elbow.

He stood quite still; fighting nausea. He saw a man glance at him curiously, and quickly covered the thing up. He turned to the other parcel and unwrapped that, making sure that no one else could see what it was.

It was a part of a leg; a man's leg, with fine, fair hairs on it.

12

Parcels

Carmichael had lost every vestige of color. Roger watched him intently, and couldn't even begin to guess whether he was upset simply because of what he saw, or whether he had realized the greater significance of the discovery. No one else in the yard had any idea of what had been found.

"What do you want me to do?" Carmichael asked, and went on without waiting for an answer: "Of course Mr. Farnley will have to decide, but I can advise him of the best way of co-operating without upsetting the smooth flow of the work too much. You won't agree with me, but with so many perishables in the mail and so many parcels, it's easily a record year—anything which might hamper us must take second place to the mail."

Roger said quietly: "Have word sent round that all perishable parcels are to be brought over here, will you, especially anything with a smell of putrefaction. No need yet to tell the men what's happened. Get a couple of chaps you can trust to collect the parcels—and pick them up by the string. Don't open any more, just check the addresses and where they were posted, and handle them as little as you can. We might find fingerprints that will help. All right?"

"Yes. Yes, of course. You mean we *needn't* stop work?"

"Not yet."

Roger had an odd idea that Carmichael was blessing him, as he turned away.

He sent for the three Yard men still on duty at River Way; also for a police surgeon and for an assistant from the Police Laboratory, and superintended the collection of the parcels. There were hundreds; but those he was interested in were easy to pick out.

The body; so far as it could be assembled, was of a young man.

The hands were missing; so was the head.

The parcels had been posted at different offices throughout the west and southwest London area, the previous morning.

Preliminary medical evidence said that the dissection had been carried out skillfully but not surgically, and that the body had been exposed to a warm temperature for some time.

"Could the man have been alive forty-eight hours ago?" Roger asked the doctor. "Roughly."

"It's hard to say. Three days, yes. Two—well, I don't know."

Derek Bryant had been missing for nearly three days.

"Any way of being sure?" Roger asked.

"When we've finished the p.m. we might be able to give you a better idea," the doctor said. "Young man, fair-haired, aged about twenty-three or four. If we could find the hands I could tell you a lot more; until we do I'm guessing."

"Don't guess any more," Roger said.

He left the doctor and the laboratory assistant, and went into the small room which had been set aside for him and the newcomers from the Yard. A junior Post Office official was also with them. There were dozens of sheets of brown paper, piled up, and one of Wilberforce's men was going over them methodically with fingerprint powder. It was difficult to get prints on some, because the paper was too damp, but there were dozens on others.

"Know exactly what you're looking for?" Roger asked him.

"Any print common to all the parcels."

"That's right," Roger said, "thanks." He turned to the official, a youngish, bookish man who looked awed at his company. "Sorry to harass you like this today, but we've a problem we can't solve without your help." As an opening sentence, that seldom failed. "We want to find out which Post Office these parcels came from and, if possible, the time they were posted. What are the chances?"

He didn't think they were good. No one could be expected to remember these particular parcels; in the beginning, they must have been like any others to look at. There seemed nothing remarkable about the paper or the string, the shape or the method of packing. One or two, which had been better preserved, would have passed as innocuous anywhere.

"We can get some data," the young man said confidently. His round, thin-framed glasses gave him an old-fashioned look. "Depends how they were stamped. Some offices have machines; they stamp the postage paid and the date, and *some* stamp the time on, too. At the little Sub Post Offices where they put on adhesive stamps and slap a rubber stamp over to cancel them we can't tell very much. But you'll certainly get some facts, sir."

"Fine!" Roger turned to one of the Yard men. "You lend a hand with that, make out a list of the Post Offices and the times as far as possible. See if there's any kind of pattern." He didn't add that it looked as if someone had gone out with a huge load of parcels and had posted two or three at different offices; too many of the same kind would have been noticeable.

He went back to the Yard.

On his desk was a photograph of Derek Bryant, a happy-looking young man with fair hair, aged twenty-two, about the height and build of the dismembered body.

The telephone bell rang.

"West speaking," Roger said.

"Hallo, Handsome," said Detective Inspector Turnbull, in his most booming voice. "Just picked up a bit of news for you; what you'd do without me I just can't tell."

"I could tell you what I could do with the time we're wasting."

"Okay, okay," said Turnbull, bluffly. "I'm across the river at Battersea. Derek Bryant's motorbike's been picked up in a wrecker's yard. No sign of Bryant. The Divisional boys are working on it and they'll send a report straight to you."

"Thanks," said Roger, "that's a help."

He sat at the desk, smoking, and staring at the

window. The clouds were much lower, and they still had the yellowy gray look that snow clouds often had. It wasn't actually snowing, but it was much colder in the office than for several days. The windows were tightly closed, and the traffic noises came in muffled and distant.

From Derek Bryant it was a flash of thought to Mrs. Bryant and May Harrison.

What would they feel about that?

It was almost as if the fates had singled them out for a buffeting which would cause them so much harm that they would probably never recover.

But until the hands and the head were found, no one could be sure.

There was another problem. Mrs. Bryant for certain, Micky probably and May Harrison possibly would know if Derek had any distinguishing marks on the body. Once he put the question they would guess the truth, and if his fears were justified that would mean more anguish in the family. He wouldn't ask about body marks until later. It didn't make all that difference at the moment; knowing that the body was Derek's didn't affect the issue yet.

He got up, slid into his coat and carried his hat, and went downstairs. At the top of the steps, the duty sergeant was beating his arms across his chest, although it wasn't really as cold as that in here, even with the doors opening and closing all the time.

"Going to get it," the duty sergeant said.

"Nice for the kids," said Roger.

Two or three flakes of snow were drifting about as he reached his car. He didn't give it more thought, but got in and drove toward River Way again; but this time he passed the Post Office building. Fifteen minutes after leaving the Yard, he was in Clapp Street. A policeman stood near the Bryants' house, but there were only two or three other people in the street, only one standing outside the house itself.

Roger pulled up outside Number 72.

The decorated tree was still in the window, and none of the front-room decorations had been taken down. There were five full days to Christmas. He knocked at the door, and heard a child saying: "Mummy, someone here."

You had to hand it to Kath Bryant.

She had a dust cap round her pretty hair, and wore a blue apron, shorter than her black frock. Her sleeves were rolled up and she reminded Roger of Janet on a busy morning. She had an air of bustle, too, was obviously surprised to see him, and stood quite still for a moment, as if shocked. It was the first time she had acted like that, and it puzzled him.

Hadn't she recognized him?

Or didn't she want to see him?

He said: "Good morning, Mrs. Bryant, I hope this isn't a bad time to call."

"No, of course not," she said, rather too quickly. "Please come in." She put a hand down to Tim, the three-year-old, and held his hand as if she wanted comfort from somewhere. "You—you don't mind that I'm in the middle of my housework."

"It would be odd if you weren't."

She said quickly: "I'm all right if I can keep busy, but the moment I stop, it all comes over me." That was better; but Roger couldn't forget the way she had looked, couldn't stop asking himself whether she had been sorry that he had come; even a little scared. "I suppose I shall be all right, as time goes on. It's the season which makes it worse than it would be, I suppose. The children break up from school tomorrow, and—and they try so hard *not* to look forward to Christmas Day, but how can I stop them?"

Roger said slowly: "I don't think I should try. Will you spend Christmas at home or with friends?"

The lift of her chin held pride and defiance.

"At home," she answered firmly. "The neighbors have been wonderful, but they have their own families and it's the busiest time of the year. I—but you didn't come to hear my gossiping." She led the way into the front room, with its paper chains and its holly. It was spotlessly clean, and the brasses in the fireplace sparkled. "Is—is there any more news?"

"No," said Roger. "We still don't know what it's all about, but we do know that a killer's at large, and we're scared of what he might do next if we don't get our hands on him."

Kath Bryant didn't speak.

"After the way he attacked Miss Harrison—have you heard how she is this afternoon?"

"No, but Micky's going to see her soon," Mrs. Bryant said; "the nurses *thought* she recognized him when he was there last night."

"The morning's report was good," Roger told her. In fact it had been middling good. "We're more puzzled than ever about the man who came here and attacked Miss Harrison," he went on. "We just can't find a reason for it. And it's possible that

130

something that your husband said or did in the last few days, perhaps even in the last few weeks, might help us to find out." When Mrs. Bryant didn't answer, Roger continued: "Have you any idea at all where he got that hundred pounds from?"

She shook her head, firmly.

"Is there anything you can tell us?" Roger demanded.

She hesitated for a fraction of a second, just long enough for him to sense the doubt in her, to suspect that she wasn't being wholly frank.

She was thinking: "I can't tell him about the key until I know what Tom wanted it for."

She knew that she would probably never find out, and also knew that she was trying to find an excuse for holding it back, but—why *had* Tom wanted it?

"I just can't tell him about the key," she thought, "I couldn't bear it if they tried to say that Tom—"

She didn't finish, even when talking to herself.

"No," she said to Roger, "I just can't imagine."

He felt sure that she was lying.

It wasn't difficult to imagine why. Every other person who had given any thought to Bryant's murder must have wondered why; and so wondered whether he was playing a crooked game and had been killed for his part in it. That dread might well be in his wife's mind.

She was no fool.

She had a great strength of will, too; that had been obvious almost from the beginning. Now she stood there with a kind of defiance, the "No, I just can't imagine" still on her lips. It wouldn't be easy to break her down, and Roger wasn't yet sure that he must try.

But if she had reason to suspect why the thief had come, her soldier son might guess too. Micky would be much easier to handle.

"Well, I needn't worry you any more now, Mrs. Bryant," Roger said, "but if you do recall anything, even an old phrase or so which would be worth our following up, please tell us at once. It might be vital. It might even make a difference between catching the murderer and failing to catch him— and I hate the idea of him running around loose." He let that sink in, but she showed no reaction; now that she had decided on her course, she would steer it unwaveringly.

"I understand fully," she said.

Roger went out, and as he turned to look at her and Tim, who wandered back to her, Tim was stretching out a hand and pointing.

"Snow?" he said, in a questioning voice.

"That's right, darling," Kath Bryant said firmly. "It's snowing."

She closed the door.

Roger had been inside for less than twenty minutes, but it had changed the face of the narrow street, giving it a beauty which seemed to belong to another world. The snow was falling fast, and there was already a covering on the road, the pavements, the roofs; and; the window ledges were touched with it, the lamp posts had a soft white covering, so had the post box at a corner. The footsteps of two children who were walking toward him hardly sounded.

"Now I wonder what's the best way to work on

young Micky?" Roger asked himself, as he sat at the wheel and started the engine.

Being so near, he went home for lunch. Janet was alone, the boys having a midday meal at school. She had been about to have a boiled egg but quickly fried eggs and sausages.

Roger was almost sluggish when he left.

Along the Embankment every vehicle now left clear tracks in the snow. The Post Office yard, clearer than it had been last time he had passed, was filmed with white. He turned in. Carmichael was still on the job, and he deliberately looked another way, but Roger hadn't come to see him. He went to the office which had been set aside for the police, and found the earnest young official sitting at a desk, pencil in hand, a diagram in the other. There was the Fingerprints man too, sitting with three sheets of soiled brown paper in front of him, a large pile on one side, a smaller pile on the other.

Everyone jumped up at sight of Roger.

"What've we got?" He liked the look of excitement in the eyes even of an old and staid sergeant.

"Remarkable thing, sir," said the young Post Office official. "I could hardly believe it when I first discovered it. The offices coincide with one of our collecting rounds. You know how we do it, don't you? We have certain rounds, say twenty or thirty offices to call on; you see the really vital thing is to keep the flow of parcels and letters moving. So the whole of the southwest district on this side of the river is divided into rounds—see." He pointed eagerly to a map on the wall where the main Post Offices were marked in red and the smaller ones in blue. Colored lines were drawn from dot to dot, each line a different color.

"We give each round a number, sir," the official went on with that welcome eagerness, "and we always send to each Post Office for specimen stamp-machine franking. So we can check where the parcels came from, you see; there's always a flaw, same as in typewriters. And of the twenty-one pieces of paper with a franking machine gummed slip stuck on, *all* are on Round G. We've got impressions of rubber stamps used at the smaller offices, too; most of them have a fault in, as you said. They fit in the gaps. *All* those parcels were posted on Round G, undoubtedly."

Roger felt excitement rising. "Now let's find out who collected from Round G yesterday morning," he said. "But before we do—" he broke off, looking very grave—partly to hide his excitement, partly for effect.

"Yes?" The word popped out.

"Not a word to anyone—not to Mr. Carmichael or the Head Postmaster or anyone at all, until we give you permission."

"Oh, *I* won't blab," the lad assured him. "You don't want it known what we're finding out, then?"

"Not yet."

"Well, I'll have to ask a few questions," the official said. "The best way is for me to slip out to one or two of the offices and have a word with the postmasters or the clerks in charge. They'll remember who did the rounds—anyway they always get a signature for every consignment. Could be one of our own vans or a private hire, of course, and—"

"Just try to check," Roger urged.

"Like a shot," the youngster promised, and went hurrying off.

Wilberforce's middle-aged fingerprint expert was very different from the large youth who had been with Wilberforce on the first night; he had finished checking the parcel wrappings, and was sitting and smoking. Although he had used a lot of gray dusting powder, hardly any showed on the desk or on his clothes; but the top sheets of brown wrapping paper were smeared. He'd taken photographs of them all, and his little camera was hung over his shoulder.

The other Yard men were old stagers; nothing was likely to excite them, but one said: "This means someone from this Post Office posted those parcels, Mr. West."

"Almost certainly," Roger agreed.

"Hell of a ruddy business," the man grunted, and looked at the fingerprints expert. "Anything on your side, Tommy?"

That saved Roger the trouble of asking.

Tommy said very quietly: "Yes." He handed Roger a slip of paper. "Thirty-one sheets of paper in all. On twenty-six there are sets or part sets of identical prints, and there are none on the other— but those parcels were dampest, and the prints didn't show up properly. Twenty-six good enough for you, sir?"

Roger said: "I don't think we need worry about the five, Tommy." He was reading the notes which the expert had made in a thin, neat hand. They stated simply what the man had already said, and added: *Thumb prints all show a slight scar. All prints follow the Tented Arch pattern.*

The prints on the shaft of the hammer; on the

glass; and on Simm's van, all carried those same characteristics—and the same fragment in every case.

"We want to know everyone on G round yesterday morning and when we know we want everyone's prints taken," Roger said grimly, "and it's got to be done in a hurry."

Carmichael, who had now been told, shook his head worriedly.

"It's easy to say, but not so easy to do, Mr. West. I am not being obstructive, but we had ten or twelve vans and lorries on that round yesterday, and each lorry had two or three temporary workers. Not all of them have reported for work today, and some have been transferred to smaller offices to help clear accumulations of mail. After all, the mail *must* go through. Making sure we get all of the people you want is going to be extremely difficult. If it could wait just for a day or two—" he broke off, and gave a watery little smile. "No. Of course not! Well, young Ryde's got the list, he's at your disposal, and all I can do is wish you luck."

Roger went straight to Fingerprints when he reached the Yard. Wilberforce was there, with four big photographs in front of him—the same fragment of a print enlarged almost to the size of a man's hand.

"So they look odd to you, too," Roger said.

Wilberforce hardly troubled to glance round.

"Don't get it," he said, "unless this chap's got himself some plastic or rubber gloves which fi skin tight, and there's a hole in one that he doesn' know about." Wilberforce scratched his head

136

"Needn't be a hole proper, could be just a flaw. Like you often get in a toy balloon when it's blown up." He deliberated. "That could be the answer. There's one thing that supports the idea, Handsome. The first prints are in reverse not from the natural skin oils, but on a greasy surface. The oil on the hammer, the butter on the glass, grease on the lock of the van door. This brown paper's different—looks as if he'd got oil on his hands, and the pressure he used in doing the parcels up made the impression through the thin rubber or plastic."

Roger didn't comment.

"Okay," Wilberforce said, "so you don't believe it."

Roger grinned.

"I'd believe anything you say, Willie! Don't see what other answer we can find. I'll get the lab to experiment with thin rubber and plastic. That ghoulish look you saw on my face was about something different."

"What?"

"I was thinking what a mess there must have been when the killer dismembered his victim," Roger said.

"Sometimes I'm glad my job's just fingerprints," said Wilberforce. "Where are you going now?"

"Back to River Way," said Roger. "After I've started the ball rolling in the search for the operating room where the beast did his cutting up."

It was then half past three in the afternoon.

13

A Message for Micky

Micky Bryant reached the hospital in Chelsea a little after two o'clock that day. He realized only vaguely that everyone who saw him recognized him, and that everything possible was done to make it easy for him. Receptionist, porter, nurses, all exerted themselves to help. So did the Sister, in her small office near a block of private wards. The smell of antiseptics was everywhere; the Sister was almost frightening in starched white cap and starched white collar, but her smile put Micky completely at ease.

"Well, I think we've some cheerful news for you," she said, "although nothing to get excited about yet. Miss Harrison seems to be more herself, and when she woke after a morning sleep she seemed to have some idea where she was. But if she doesn't recognize you, don't harass her, will you?"

"No, I promise you I won't."

"Let's go along, then," said the Sister.

She was much taller than the lad, and looking

down she couldn't fail to see his pallor, or the hurt look in his gray eyes. She felt as every nurse who had seen him had; as every neighbor felt; as his mother did: that there must be some way of helping him, but it was difficult to put a finger on the method.

He looked more lost than frightened.

May was in a private ward.

A woman in nurse's uniform sat in an easy chair by the window, but more often than not she had a beat in the West End of London, which she shared with a male constable. Under her apron she had a notebook and pencil. She stood up quickly, also feeling a deep compassion for Micky.

The Sister said softly: "Is she still asleep?"

"Yes." Whispered.

Micky heard them, without quite realizing what they were saying. He stared at May. Next to his mother, she was the only woman whom he really knew. In a way, she was more like his sister than just Derek's girl. Lying like that, with an old flannelette nightdress pulled high at the neck so that the bruises didn't show, it was hard to believe that there was anything the matter with her. Her eyes were closed, and she had beautiful lashes. She had a better color, too, and her pretty hair had been combed and brushed. Her arms were underneath the clothes, so that only her head and face showed.

Micky kept swallowing a lump in his throat, but it wouldn't go. He took a step toward the bed, then another, then a third; and he faltered at that. Tears welled up in his eyes, and the women could hear the gulping noise that he made, as well as see those tears, but neither of them spoke.

Micky didn't go too near.

139

Suddenly, he turned his head.

"She will be all right, won't she?" he asked, and there was passion in his voice. "She will get well again?"

"Perfectly well," the Sister said.

"But are you *sure*?"

"It may take a little time, but she'll be perfectly well again before long," the Sister declared, and went on more quickly: "Don't speak so loudly, we don't want to wake—"

She broke off.

"She *is* awake," breathed Micky.

He moved as if he was impelled by some force that he couldn't withstand, rushing him toward the bed. The Sister was unable to restrain him. He didn't thrust himself at May, but stopped by the bed, his hands stretched out toward her, and the tears quivering on his eyelashes.

May's eyes opened.

She was looking at the ceiling, and stared upward for a few seconds, as if she didn't realize that she was lying in bed. It was a long time before she moved, and probably she would not have done so but for the sob which forced itself from Micky's lips. She turned her head slowly. She wasn't smiling, but her lips were relaxed in what looked very much like a smile.

She looked straight into his eyes.

"May," choked Micky. "May, it's me, it's Micky."

She didn't turn away. She frowned a little, as if she didn't understand why his lips trembled or the way he looked at her.

Her lips moved.

"Where is Derek?" she asked. "You're not Derek."

*   *   *

"Yes, thank you very much, I shall be perfectly all right," Micky said firmly. "I'm much better now, and I'm only sorry that I made a fool of myself." He didn't smile, and he kept his voice very steady; as if he had drilled himself into hiding his emotion. "It must be because I've had rather an upsetting time."

The Sister said briskly: "Yes, that must be it. Are you sure you won't have another cup of tea?"

"No, thank you. I must get back to my mother, now."

"Yes, of course," said the Sister. "Tell her that I don't think it will be long before Miss Harrison remembers everyone again."

"Thank you," said Micky. "Thanks very much."

He sounded, he looked and he felt very young. But he walked smartly along the rubber-floored corridors and down the stairs and as smartly past the reception desk, without looking right or left, and still smartly down to the foot of the steps. Nearby was his pedal bicycle. He mounted the machine and cycled off, and one of the porters watched him, frowning; the lad hardly seemed to be looking where he was going.

Just round the corner, Micky pulled into the curb and sat on the saddle, one foot on the curb, the other on a pedal. He couldn't keep the scalding tears away, but at least he could make sure that no one saw them. He dabbed fiercely at his eyes with a handkerchief, and averted his face whenever anyone came along.

He felt better, after a few minutes.

"Don't be a fool," he muttered, "don't be a helpless *kid.* I'm grown up, I'm in the Army, I'm nearly *nineteen.*"

His jaws hurt, where he had gritted them so tightly.

"If I could find the devil who did it," he said in a harsh voice, "I'd kill him with my own hands."

He didn't know how absurd it sounded. He didn't know how theatrical he looked. There was no one to see him at that moment. He dabbed his eyes again, and felt sure that he was over the paroxysm, then cycled off. He was better, and felt equally sure that he wouldn't break down again. He had good news, really, because he'd actually heard May speak, and the only snag was that Derek hadn't turned up.

He was less worried about Derek than anyone else was; Derek was one of the permanent people in life, like—

Only when he reached the corner did he realize that it was snowing, and he looked about him with a sudden excitement, a legacy from his so recent childhood. Why, it was getting quite thick! He felt the tires crunch through the snow, and saw the difference it made to the streets, the houses, the grayness. Oddly, he was almost light-hearted.

It took him nearly half an hour to reach home; yet he had lost ten minutes just outside the hospital. The policeman who had been on duty when he had left was still there; and there was the now familiar look of compassion. Micky didn't realize or recognize it.

"Your mother's still in," the policeman said.

"Anyone with her?"

"Only Mrs. Trentham."

"Oh, that's good," said Micky. Rosa Trentham

was the one neighbor he could face now. He braced himself and went in, reminding himself that he was taking good news. He marched straight past the little hallstand, the door of the small room, and into the kitchen. Mrs. Trentham was standing with a bread knife in her hand, calling toward the scullery:

"Here he is, Kath; I told you you were worrying yourself for nothing. Hallo, Micky, how is she?" The question came quickly and bluffly; and it helped the boy.

His mother appeared at the kitchen door.

Micky's eyes were bright.

"I saw her; she looks fine," he said, and then had to overdo it. "She looks lovely, she does really, and Sister says she's better. She—she woke up, too."

His mother said swiftly, eagerly: "Did she recognize you?"

"Well," said Micky awkwardly, "not exactly, but she knew I was a man. As a matter of fact, she asked for Derek; she knew I wasn't Derek, anyhow! And honestly, she was looking fine."

"Well, what did I tell you?" asked Rosa Trentham. "If only Derek would come back—but it doesn't matter whether he does or not until she's a bit better, and he's bound to turn up. Like a bad penny—they always do. Eh, Micky? Want a cup of tea, son?"

"No, thanks, they gave me some at the hospital."

"Well, we'll have one," said Mrs. Trentham. "Turn the kettle up, Kath. And what about those few oddments from the shop? If you don't get them this afternoon you won't be able to get that mince-meat done tonight, and as you insist on doing it ..."

*　　　*　　　*

The snow came down only lightly during the night, and there was a thin carpet which quickly melted in the roads under the assault of gravel, salt and traffic. Roger was at the Yard early, with paper work in plenty but little else. The one thing he did not look forward to was the funeral of Tom Bryant, but he was there.

Snow still lay thinly on the cemetery grass and on the mounds which covered the recently filled graves. It was bitterly cold. Micky was with his mother, but none of the other children had been allowed to come. There were hundreds of mourners and masses of flowers; neighbors, work mates, friends from the church, from clubs and organizations. The funeral service had a kind of frozen solemnity.

The only time that Kath Bryant broke down was at the graveside, as she dropped her wreath into the earth to which her husband had returned.

Roger drove away from the cemetery, and went to River Way. The snow made traffic jams and indescribable confusion. Carmichael was like an automaton; Farnley looked positively ill. Turnbull was there, but even he was subdued.

"Checked every van in the place, every drawer, desk, key and locker," he said, "and we haven't found that print again."

"Keep looking," Roger said. "Everything laid on to guard valuables and registered parcels?"

"Every damned thing."

"Good," Roger said.

He went out in the yard, talked to one or two

temporary workers, and then to Kilby, who had nothing to report, except: "I was out this morning with the van driver Simm, sir."

"How does he rate?"

"Works very hard," said Kilby, "and made up half an hour—we went for a drink."

"Like that, is it?" Roger said. "He probably did that the other day, too."

He was driving back to the Yard with his radio receiver on, when he heard his own name coming over. He flicked the transmitter on.

"West calling."

"Message just come in, Mr. West," the radio operator said. "May Harrison's recovered her memory sir."

Roger said: "Fine!" He switched off and swung round at the next corner; and he reached the hospital in ten minutes. He didn't wait to have his name sent up but reached the Sister's office on the private floor.

The Sister said firmly: "The doctor's orders are emphatic, Chief Inspector. Miss Harrison is not to be questioned for longer than two minutes."

"That'll be enough," Roger said.

He went into the ward. The police nurse was sitting in her corner, and May Harrison sitting up in bed. She looked quite normal. Obviously she recognized him, and yet wasn't at all perturbed.

Surely she would have been if she knew that her assailant had been Derek.

Roger said quietly: "I'm very glad you're better, Miss Harrison. Just one essential question, then I won't bother you again."

"I'll tell you anything I can," she promised.

145

"Did you see the face of the man who attacked you?"

"No, not even a glimpse," she said.

He found it hard to believe that she was lying.

He found it harder to tell her that Derek was still missing.

He was glad that she was to go back to Clapp Street that evening.

Nothing would break; nothing went their way; but it couldn't go on like this, Roger tried to persuade himself. The whole picture was of gloom. A blizzard, raging in the north and midlands, was on its way south. It was bitterly cold, and had been as fruitless a day as Roger had known for a long time. But next morning there was a little break in the clouds, when Johnny Silver rang up.

"Got a bit of a line on young Derek Bryant," he said. "Not in person, but he's cropped up in a different way. He's been to Didi Ames's place several times. Carmichael had competition!"

"Sure about that?" Roger demanded sharply.

"Positive. There's a nosy-parker widower in a house opposite. I've more."

"What?"

"His father's been a visitor there."

"*Tom* Bryant?" This was almost unbelievable.

"That's how I got on to it. Had a word with the widower in the street; I'd picked him out as a know-all. He was full of importance because he'd actually *seen* the murdered man."

"When was it?"

"Two or three days before the murder. I can't pin him down any closer."

"Keep trying," urged Roger. "Anything on Didi Ames?"

"She cold-shouldered everyone last night," said Silver. "I didn't get a chance."

"Was Carmichael at the night club?"

"No, and he didn't visit her, either, went straight to his Paddington place, and she went straight to St. John's Wood."

"I wonder if they've quarreled," Roger mused.

He rang off—and immediately the telephone rang again. There was hardly time to think even about Tom Bryant and Didi Ames.

Kilby didn't quite know what had happened to him, but he did know that the Bryant job wasn't just another investigation. He'd never felt a crime so deeply, for it gave him an almost personal hatred for the killer. He had another driving force, too. West had given him a pretty free hand, and he wanted to justify it.

He watched every move of Carmichael and Simm. He found excuses for going down to the maintenance department, which was near some cloakrooms, and where some of the old tunnels were used as store rooms. He put his mind to work on every aspect of the job, but it was an accident which put him on the right track.

He found some sheets of brown wrapping paper, used for rewrapping damaged parcels, and they were identical with those in which the pieces of the body had been wrapped.

He could have telephoned the Yard then.

He didn't, but went to the store rooms. The brown paper was in one of the old tunnels, and the door wasn't kept locked. He had only one hope, there: to find the familiar print. He switched on the light, and began to look round, with the door ajar.

It was a low-roofed tunnel, with racks at the walls, and there was a strong smell of disinfectant. Kilby, head bent to save himself from hitting it on the ceiling, kept sniffing. Why use so much disinfectant in a stationery store room?

He went toward the far end, and saw that the floor and the walls there had been swabbed down. With an almost choking sense of excitement, he went down on one knee to look at a stain in a corner. Men were walking about outside in the passage, and someone was hammering; he didn't give that a thought.

He didn't know that a man came creeping in until he heard a faint sound behind him. On his knee, he tried to twist round.

He was too late. A blow smashed onto the back of his head, and he slumped down....

He knew nothing of being dragged behind the stationery racks, and being left there; or of the light being switched off, and the door closed and locked.

It did not surprise Roger that there was no message from Kilby, who wouldn't report unless he had news. Roger hardly gave the sergeant a thought, but tried to make up his mind whether to leave Johnny Silver to deal with Didi Ames, or whether to tackle her himself.

He gave Silver one more night.

*   *   *

In the house in Clapp Street there was a semblance of normality. Although taking it easy, May was much more herself. There was a round of shopping and the inevitable extra work for Kath Bryant. Micky, with a month's compassionate leave, ran most of the errands. He liked to be out. In different ways, the expression in his mother's and in May's eyes hurt him.

About the time of the attack on Kilby, Micky cycled toward the Wandsworth Bridge Road and the shops, armed with a list and a shopping bag. The sound of the tires crunching through the snow, now an inch or so thick, was pleasant and in its way thrilling. He felt much more normal. He turned the corner of the street, noticing a man standing near a lamp post a little further along, with a cloth cap on, and his coat collar turned up. He saw the man step forward, and heard him call:

"Say, you."

Micky braked cautiously, and the wheels didn't skid. He turned the front wheel toward the curb.

"Want something?" He couldn't see the other's face very well, he was so huddled up in his coat and the hat brim was pulled so low over his eyes. He was a youth, not a man.

"You Micky Bryant?"

"That's right."

"Got a message for you."

"For *me?*"

"S'right. Message from chap named Derek."

Micky caught his breath. "My—my brother?"

"S'right."

Micky swung his leg over the crossbar and asked

149

eagerly: "Where is he, do you know? I want to see him ever so badly."

"He's in a jam."

"*What?*"

"In a jam, in a hole, bit of a squeeze, tight corner, see."

"In—in a *jam!*"

"That's what I said. Doesn't want anyone to know where he is, and there's something you can do to help him. Says he's sure you will; if you don't it might mean a lot more trouble for your Ma."

The elation faded but the excitement remained.

"What—what does he want me to do?"

"Got any cash?"

"Well, not much, I—I've got a few pounds."

"He wants you to take as much cash as you can lay your hands on, and go to Baker Street Station —you know. The entrance at the corner. What time can you be there?"

Micky said stammeringly: "I don't know, I—"

"Wouldn't let your own brother down, would you?" That was a sneer.

"No, but I—"

"What time can you be there? How about going right away?"

"I can't, I've some things to get for my mother, but—is it very bad?"

"Derek thinks it is," sneered the youth. His eyes were more clearly visible, now, in the gathering dusk; they glinted as if they were nearly black. "They're trying to pin a murder rap on him, and just for a few quid you can help him beat it."

"I'll get there as soon as I can, but it can't be until six o'clock," Micky said desperately. "Will that be all right?"

150

"It'll have to be. Know the station?"

"Isn't it near Madame Tussaud's?"

"Yeh." The youth leaned forward a little. Now Micky saw that he had a thin, pointed nose and a mustache which wasn't real; it couldn't be. "Okay, six sharp, see. Don't say a word to no one. Bring as much nicker as you can, and don't forget your brother needs help."

"I—I don't think I can bring much more than ten pounds," Micky said. "I'll try, though. If I don't hurry now I'll be late."

"Then hurry, chum," the youth said, "and not a word to anyone, see. Don't split to your Ma or anyone else, not if you want to help Derek."

"I—I won't."

"You'd better not," the youth said.

He turned and slouched away, making no sound in the snow which was now over an inch thick, and falling fast.

It was then half past four.

Micky was followed from the corner of Wandsworth Bridge Road, although he did not know it. The youth followed him; and made sure that no one else took note of the way Micky went. It did not occur to him to find out if he was being watched as he rode through the driving snow toward the Post Office near the library. When he got in, he groaned. It was bulging with people in front of the counter and parcels behind it. Half a dozen girls seemed to be working with frantic rhythm. The *bang bang bang* of rubber stamps seemed ceaseless. So did the murmur of voices. It was stuffy and hot. It was wet underfoot. Most people were grumbling at the delay, but there were fewer at the Pensions and Savings Bank counter than anywhere else. It took Micky ten minutes to draw out ten pounds from his savings book, all that he could on demand. Now, he had twelve pounds.

The saddle of his bicycle was covered with snow when he got outside. There was a lot of slush at the curbs. Rumbling buses crunched over this as they went along. Cars were going slowly, and every now and again there was the *clank clank clank* of tire chains. Older people on the pavements walked very cautiously, and several slipped. Children at one corner were giggling as they stood with snowballs in their hands. A man, passing, muttered: "Damned kids," but no one stopped them. Lights from the cars, the shop windows and the lamp standards showed how heavily the snow was falling.

Micky thought: "I'm going to be late."

He knew the way across London well, for in the summers of his schooldays he had spent a lot of time at Lord's. He knew that road conditions would be very bad, but probably easier on the side roads. He didn't realize that another youth followed him, on a bicycle. All he worried about was keeping his balance, keeping the snow out of his eyes, and getting to the rendezvous in time. He couldn't move the gauntlets off his wrists to see what the time was, but every now and again he passed a public clock, or one outside a shop: it was ten minutes to six when he was within sight of Baker Street.

He reached the station at seven minutes to.

Streams of people were hurrying toward the subways which took them out of the snowstorm, as if they were flakes which melted into the semidarkness of the station itself. They disappeared by the hundred; by the thousand. Micky stood at one side, trying to see the faces of the people, expecting to see Derek, wondering desperately—as he had from the beginning—what was really the matter with Derek. The suspicion that *Derek* might have had something to do with the attack on May actually entered his head.

He shied away from it, and all that it would imply.

The clock in sight moved visibly, although snow had gathered on its face.

Five to six—five past six.

Well, at least he had been on time, and he couldn't help it if Derek was late.

"So you made it." It wasn't Derek, but the youth who had accosted him round the corner from Clapp Street. He was dressed in the same clothes, but his cap and his shoulders were thick with snow. His shoulders were still hunched, and it was difficult to see his features clearly, for the peak of the cap hid his eyes.

Micky jumped round. "Yes, I—I was here early. Where—where's Derek?"

"I'll take you to him," the youth said. "Leave your bike; no one will run away with it on a night like this; we'll take a cab. That's if we can find one." It didn't seem to occur to him that taking a cab was almost unique in Micky's experience.

One came up, its sign glowing, to announce that it was empty. They got in. Micky sat back, unsteadily, fingers nearly frozen, nose frozen, teeth chattering with the cold. The other youth kept drawing at the cigarette until the ash got so long that it dropped downward; and when the taxi stopped suddenly, it fell off.

They turned several corners before they got out, at another corner. The youth paid the cabby off, and then took Micky's arm. The snow, now inches thick, muffled every sound they made. Other people coming toward them moved with the same uncanny silence; a few held umbrellas; most of them walked with bowed shoulders.

They turned another corner.

Micky thought: "Why didn't we come right to the door?" He didn't give that much thought, he was too cold and scared; scared because of the danger to Derek.

Then, they reached a house. It stood back from the road and in its own grounds. A car was parked just along the drive. Lights showed at several windows, and shone upon the snow. Some bushes looked like huge white mushrooms. The noise of traffic behind them vanished, and now they could hear the sounds of their own muffled progress. It seemed a long way to the front door, and the snow gathered on Micky's boots, so that he seemed to be walking on cobbles, but they reached the door at last, and the youth just turned the handle and thrust it open. As he went in, a bell rang somewhere.

He closed the door.

"First floor," he said.

"*Is* Derek here?"

The youth didn't speak, but gripped Micky's arm. He was much stockier and much more powerful than Derek, but there was no physical fear in Micky's mind then, just uneasiness. They reached the first-floor landing, and a door opened as they reached it.

A big man stood there.

There was nothing frightening in that; the frightening thing was the mask he had over his face.

It was an ordinary *papier maché* mask, with a shiny red nose and shiny cheeks, gaps for the mouth and gaps for the eyes; and yet it was frightening. The shock was so great that Micky didn't move, after a first instinctive pace backward. He wasn't allowed to go too far back. The youth gripped his arm and thrust him forward, and the man with the child's mask on took his wrist and pulled him into the hall.

The door closed.

"Look—look here—" Micky began.

"Shut your trap," the man said. His voice was muffled behind his mask, and his grip was tight and painful. "You've got a job to do."

Something happened to Micky.

Until that moment he had been edgy and scared and fearful for Derek. Now, he knew that this was a trick, although he didn't know what it was about. The youth had lied and the man was out to terrify him.

Micky didn't say a word, but twisted his left arm free from the youth, and wrenched himself out of the big man's grip. He grew from a child who looked as if he was masquerading in uniform, to a menacing fighting machine. As he twisted, he made the big man cry out. He hacked at the youth's shins and, when the big man struck at him, he ducked beneath the blow and rammed his fists, left, right, left, right, into the other's stomach. The man gave ground, gasping, and the mask slipped to one side, but it didn't show all of his face. The youth was crouching against the wall, his cap on the floor, his face clearly visible for the first time, with its thin features and the bushy false mustache.

Micky swung round to the door.

He pulled at the knob of the Yale lock, felt it slide back—and heard a movement behind him. He saw the big man leaping again, but the real danger came from the youth, who had a stick in his hand.

A stick?

Whatever it was glinted in the light as he brought it down on the back of Micky's head.

A C.I.D. man, watching the house where Didi Ames lived, saw the two youths arrive, and made a note in his book. That was all. The snow made it impossible to move quickly or to get a full view of the caller. The detective did not know and could not easily find out whether the youths had gone to the woman's flat, but he knew that one of the pair lived in another flat in the house. So this was probably nothing to do with Deirdre Ames.

14

Offer to Micky

Micky Bryant wasn't sure whether he lost consciousness or not. He felt the vicious blow, and lost all physical strength. The pain was agonizing. He saw strange lights. He knew that he fell. He thought that he was being picked up, but that might have been in a dream. The lights seemed to be going round and round, and there were unfamiliar noises in his ears.

The light grew steadier.

He opened his eyes a fraction. They didn't really hurt, and now, seen through his lashes, the light was misty. He heard a sound, without being quite sure what it was. He opened his eyes wider, but could only see a coal fire burning in a large grate, an armchair opposite him, thick carpet, a small table, a magazine, a box of chocolates and a bottle on a table—but he heard the sound again.

He was lying on a couch.

He jerked his head round, and the sudden movement hurt.

He forgot the hurt.

157

A girl came in. He didn't think "girl"; he didn't think anything, for he was completely surprised. She was lovely. She was rather small, and wore a white gown, a frilly kind of thing, which covered her shoulders but didn't hide much. It looked like the meringue on cakes. The billowy, frilly material covered her arms, but they looked almost bare. Her fingernails were scarlet and shiny.

She was *lovely*.

So soft-looking.

She saw that he was awake, and stopped for a moment, with her arms raised a little in front of her, and then she came hurrying forward, her arms outstretched, great eyes rounded and looking very bright; almost luminous. Before he realized what was happening, she was on her knees beside him, her arms were round him, and she was holding him close. Nothing like it had ever happened to Micky Bryant. He'd had hurried cuddles and snatched kisses; there was not much that he didn't know but very little that he had experienced. Now, he was enveloped in this lovely creature, her soft arms were about him, her soft breast upon him, a sweet-smelling perfume was exciting, intoxicating. He didn't even begin to understand; he had no thought, no memory, no consciousness of anything but the bewildering present.

Then, gently, she released him so that he fell back a little on soft cushions. She looked into his eyes. His heart raced and thudded like a car which had got out of control; his lips were parted; his arms were about her, lightly and very stiff.

"Oh, what brutes they were," she breathed. "I'll never forgive them, never!" She placed her right hand at the back of his head and pressed his face

158

into her softness, so warmly, so seductively. Then, she drew back again and the full power of her blue eyes, thrown into radiance by a light touch of mascara, was close to his.

He was, in fact, a nice-looking boy.

"They would never have done it if they hadn't been drunk," she said, "but—oh, never mind them; are you feeling better?"

He managed to say: "Yes, yes, thanks." He was beginning to think now, but his thoughts were mostly confused.

"Oh, your *head!*" she exclaimed, and drew him forward again, touching his head gently with her fingers, seeing the bump, touching it enough to make it hurt; but it was exquisite pain. "Thank goodness they didn't break the skin." She let him go again, and stood up. "Would you like a whisky, or do you think a cup of coffee would be better? Or tea?"

"I—I don't want anything." Reaction suddenly set in, making him almost angry. What did she think he was? A fool?

Remember, Derek was in a jam. The vital thing was to try to find a way to help his brother.

"Oh, you must have something," she insisted. She was now a few yards away from him, looking so very beautiful, her eyes alive with indignation and pretended concern. "I'll make you some coffee, I think. You'll like that and I'm sure it will help." But she didn't move. "They *must* have been drunk, and of course they're so angry and—and you're Derek Bryant's brother, aren't you?"

"Suppose I am."

"Why, I can tell you are!" she said. In spite of the antagonism which had taken possession of him, he couldn't fail to feel attracted, to be keenly aware of her beauty and her appeal. "I feel I can trust you not to pass on anything that I tell you in confidence," she went on. "Will you *promise?*"

He mustn't let her fool him, remember. He must help Derek. But if she thought she *was* fooling him, he might learn more. He didn't have to quarrel or be rude to her.

"You know what men are," she said, and squeezed his hand. "I suppose Derek's no better and no worse than the rest of them. He didn't tell me that he had a fiancée. I didn't know until I read about it in the newspapers. He said that he was passionately in love with me!" She gave a little smile, she looked a little sad, and she paused to give Micky time to take in the significance of all this.

Micky knew that Derek was a fool where girls were concerned. May didn't know that, but he was.

"So naturally I trusted him. After all he is a nice-looking boy, isn't he?" The woman paused again for a moment, and then added thoughtfully: "I suppose May Harrison is nice-looking, too."

"She—she's all right," Micky muttered.

"Well, if I'd only known I wouldn't have let Derek spend a lot of money on taking me about," the woman said. "We found out afterward that it was more than he could afford, and he got badly into debt. Then—well, I hate saying it but I know I can trust you not to pass it on. He stole some of my jewels."

Micky thought wildly: "Oh, no, he didn't!" Derek might play the fool with the girls, might even let May down, but steal—oh, no.

Yet he wasn't really sure, and if Derek had stolen her jewels, then her friends had every reason to try to get them back. Deep down, he was more worried than frightened, now. He wanted to ask why she hadn't gone to the police, but sensed that she would say that she didn't want to get Derek into trouble. He sensed other things, too. The youth and the men were crooks, and Derek was mixed up with them.

This woman, too.

She was watching him very closely.

"Tell me what happened," Micky said, huskily.

"Well—" She hesitated, as if genuinely reluctant to go on. "Well—he owed this money to a money-lender, you know how they put on the squeeze, and then he stole these jewels from me. I don't know whether he paid the moneylender with them or not, but I do know that something he did made him run away and hide. He's probably hiding from George, too, because George hates the sight of him. George is my brother—you can understand the way he feels, can't you?"

"Yes," Micky said. "George" would be the big man; Derek wouldn't be scared of the other one.

"Well, I lost several thousand pounds' worth of jewels," Didi Ames went on. "We know Derek put some of them away in a safe deposit, too. We know where the safe deposit is, but we can't do anything about it unless we get the key. And the key's at your house."

Micky's whole body seemed to jump.

"What?"

"Well, George and Sammy have searched every-where else, and haven't found it. Sammy went to look for it—"

Micky kept a set face, but hardly heard the next

words. So *Sammy* had broken into his house and attacked May. Sammy had nearly killed her.

"We don't know where Derek is or what he's done, but he's hiding from the police and us," the woman went on. "We wouldn't let him down, but —well, we want those jewels, don't we?"

Micky didn't pay any serious attention to the other story, but faced the fact that they wanted the key desperately.

"Where is Derek now?" he asked quietly. "Is he all right?"

"Yes, I told you—he's hiding."

"You mean, the others are keeping him prisoner," Micky said, and felt sure that he had hit upon the truth; the woman didn't deny it. "Well, I don't mind admitting I want to help Derek." And his mother, and May. "But I've got to be sure it would help him."

Didi Ames looked at him very thoughtfully.

"There's just one way to help Derek," she said at last, "and that's by getting the key. That's the only way." She went on quickly: "You're no fool, I can see that. So let me tell you something. George means to get those jewels back, or make Derek pay for it. He can frame Derek for murder, and—"

Micky flared up. "The swine! If I—"

"Listen to me," Didi Ames interrupted urgently. "There's just one way to help Derek, and that's by getting the key. Micky, you've got to believe me. George—George thought he could frighten you into getting it but—but I didn't want anyone to get hurt, so—so I made him let me handle it." She paused. "It's better this way, it really is. If you don't get the key, they'll take it out on Derek; you won't be safe anywhere you go, either."

162

Now, he believed, he had the truth. First they'd used the big stick, then the kid glove; either way they meant to get that key. If he didn't get it for them, anything might happen to Derek.

His mother couldn't stand it. He knew she couldn't. Nor May; and he couldn't stand it, either. If these were stolen jewels, what did it matter compared with making things better for Mum?

That was what he had to do.

He had heard no hint that Derek might be dead, had no reason to think that he was. Nor could he hope to separate the truth from the lies he had been told. He could only do what he believed to be right.

"If you can promise me that Derek will be okay, I'll try and get that key," he said.

Her eyes lit up.

"Oh, he'll be all right if you get it."

"How can you be so sure that the key's at my house?"

She answered simply: "Derek told us it was."

The big man was in the next room when Didi went in. He watched her with a smile that had a quality of tension, and she put her finger to her lips when she saw him. The room was carpeted, and they made no sound as they walked toward the hall, then into the small kitchen. Didi lit the gas and began to heat milk in a small, burnished saucepan, and as he watched her, she said:

"Get me that instant coffee out of the larder."

He went for it, and asked as he came back: "Think he'll go and get it?"

"Of course he'll go and get it," she said, "but not

because you scared him. He'll do it for his brother."

"You're better than I thought you were," the man sneered, "but don't forget he might get a conscience. If he should tell the police, you're going to be in trouble, aren't you?"

Didi spooned the prepared coffee into a cup very slowly and deliberately.

"I didn't want to come right out into the open with this, but you've made me," she said. "So I'm vulnerable. I'll send the kid to look for the key. You've got to make sure that, when he gets it, he can't give me or anyone else away. I don't think he'll talk first; I think he'll go and get it and come straight back here with it, but—he doesn't have to get this far, does he?"

The man said: "How ruthless can a woman be?"

She rounded on him.

"There's a fortune in this, isn't there? Am I going to be crazy enough to let a fool of a kid like that get in my way? If you'd thought of him before sending Sammy we'd be better off."

"Okay," the man said. "Shut up."

Didi didn't answer, but poured the now boiling milk onto the coffee, stirring in sugar as she poured. She was quite calm. She finished stirring, and there was a creamy froth on top of the coffee. She took some biscuits out of a tin and put them on a plate, then went toward the hall again.

"He's got to be followed all the way home and back; you've got to make absolutely sure of him," she said.

"We'll make sure of him," the man promised.

She smiled.

She was beautiful.

164

She smiled at Micky, as she went into the big room again. He hadn't moved, but looked less ill at ease. She hurried toward him, carrying the cup steadily but dropping one of the biscuits. She put coffee and biscuits on a small table close to him, and then lifted the table nearer.

"I've put plenty of sugar in," she said. "You'll feel a lot better after you've had it."

"I feel better now," Micky told her, and swung his legs off the couch, as if to prove it. "I've a bit of a headache, that's all. I'd better get a move on."

She stirred the coffee again, and handed it to him as he stood up.

"You drink this, and have a cigarette," she said. "I've squared George, and he'll give you the chance to help Derek. But if you go to the police, I wouldn't like to tell you what he'll do to Derek— *and* to you. And maybe even the kids at home."

There was a little traffic about when Micky Bryant left. It was after half past eight, and snow was falling as thickly as ever; it seemed to purr as it touched the snow already on the ground. He noticed a man come out of the doorway of a nearby house, and approach him, but the man wasn't able to move as freely as he.

He didn't go within ten yards of the man, and didn't give him a thought.

The lights of occasional cars showed the snow up clearly; so did the lights of buses. He waited at a bus stop for several minutes, and one came along with *Baker Street* among the names written on the front. He got on, and went on top. He didn't notice the motorcycle which turned out of the street he had come from, and chugged along behind the bus.

He got off at Baker Street, and he was still in a dream, still glowing in spite of the cold.

It was the sight of his bicycle, safe where he had left it, which sobered him.

His father had bought it for him two years ago.

He wondered if he really had a chance to help Derek, even if he found that key. Could he trust that woman? Was she the type who would promise the world to get what she wanted?

If he went to the police—

The woman had said they would kill Derek. And their father had been killed, so it wasn't an empty threat.

He *might* help Derek, and so help his mother and the others, if he did just what he was told.

It wasn't going to be easy. He would have a job explaining where he had been, and as he cycled back, he tried to think of the best thing to say. It was half past nine before he got home, expecting his mother to be full of anxious questions.

She wasn't there, and he felt almost guilty relief.

"Goodness knows what she would have said if she'd seen you come in like this, Micky," said Mrs. Trentham. "You look cold through. Get that coat off and change your shoes and then come and sit in front of the fire."

"No, I'm all right. Where *is* Mum?"

"She's gone to see your grandmother, and May's gone with her. Now you hurry up and put some dry clothes on, and I'll get your supper ready."

Micky was surprised that he was hungry, and was delighted that he didn't have to answer a barrage of questions.

During and after supper, all he could think

166

about was the likely hiding place for the key. It wasn't any use just looking—that might give the game away. It wouldn't be in the "study" or the desk; Sammy had searched there, and so had the police. It might be in his and Derek's room; at least he could search there.

He did, without finding the key.

After a while, he began to feel desperate. The younger children were in bed, and Mrs. Trentham left, at half past ten. He had the place to himself, but had no idea where to look. By eleven o'clock, he was in despair.

Where would Derek hide a key or anything small?

Where would he himself?

Then he remembered the little box of souvenirs, old photographs, and letters in his mother's room. Mum and Dad always hid things there, as Derek had known.

He went to look; and found the key.

15

Night Plans

Earlier that evening, Roger West picked up the receiver, said: "West speaking," and waited, looking across the desk at Johnny Silver, who had drawn up a chair on the other side. All the other C.I.s had long since gone home. In spite of the bright fire, it was cold in the office, and Silver's nose and ears were red; he had come in only half an hour ago, and hadn't thawed out.

"Might be Kilby," Roger said.

He was puzzled about Kilby's long silence, now, and Turnbull was at River Way, looking for the sergeant.

"Lot of disappearing tricks in this job," Silver said.

Roger nodded.

"Hallo, sir." It wasn't Kilby's voice. "St. John's Wood station reporting as requested." It was the man watching Didi Ames's apartment, with a dull report enlivened only by talk of the unidentified youth who'd been at the house for about two hours.

"Didn't get a good look at him, sir, because of the snow, but it wasn't Derek Bryant. Too small, sir—and a thinner chap."

"All right," said Roger. "Nothing else?"

"Miss Ames left half an hour ago, sir."

"Thanks," Roger said, and rang off. "Didi's going to do her stuff," he said to Silver. "You'd better get a move on."

"Right," said Silver.

He went off, spruce and confident, but Roger wasn't very hopeful. One got a feeling about the good and the bad angles, and he had one about Silver on this job, now. Pity.

Kilby might have been better, after all.

Kilby had vanished, into the blue.

It was too early to get worried, Roger persuaded himself; Kilby might have followed someone, seeing that the only thing to do. He wasn't a fool and wouldn't do too much on his own.

The door opened, and Turnbull came striding in.

Turnbull wasn't everyone's friend, and there were times when he and Roger clashed badly; but they got on as well as most. Now, the lion of a man was scowling, and not in one of his arrogant moods.

"Any word from Kilby?" he asked.

"No," said Roger.

"Damned queer thing," Turnbull said. "I've checked every man I can at River Way, and the last thing I can find is that he went down to the maintenance department. I know there's such a mob over there that they wouldn't notice a prize bull among them, but—"

169

"Come on," Roger said, "let's go and try again. There won't be so many people about."

When they first arrived, it looked as if he was wrong, for the yard was teeming. But inside there were fewer workers and a steadier tempo. Carmichael was at his desk, and he looked up short-sightedly, then gave a little sigh, put his pen down, and stood up.

"Is this *really* necessary?" his look said.

"No, Chief Inspector," he answered Roger's question. "Sergeant Kilby hasn't returned, to the best of my knowledge. Unfortunately when a man masquerades, as he did, I have no reason to pay special attention. However, there was a report that he was seen some time this afternoon in the maintenance department." He peered down at a note on the desk. "Ah, yes, the report was by Driver Simm."

"Simm still here?" asked Roger.

"He might be in the yard," said Carmichael, and turned to a junior. "Go and see, please."

Simm was outside.

He came striding along, massive and cocky, and dwarfing Carmichael's assistant. He grinned at Turnbull and winked at Roger.

"Flipping busies," he said, "you can tell 'em a mile off! Knew Kilby was one soon's I saw him talking to you, and giving you the wink over them parcels of prime mutton."

"Where did you last see him?" Roger interrupted sharply.

"Station'ry store," said Simm, promptly. "The door was open, he was having a dekko at some brown paper. Copper, I said to meself, just let *Mr.*

Carmichael see you, and you'll be back on the beat."

"And then?"

"Door was shut when I come back," said Simm. "I didn't see him again."

"What are we waiting for?" asked Turnbull.

Yet Roger beat him to the door.

Kilby was still unconscious, with an ugly wound at the back of his head. A hammer, taken from maintenance depot, was found near him. On it was one of the fragmentary prints, with a tented arch and scar.

At the far end of the stationery store, where the disinfectant smelled so strongly, there were patches of dried blood.

Laboratory tests soon proved that it was Group O.

The staff who had been on duty in maintenance that afternoon were now scattered all over West London. It would be useless to try to get at them tonight; the questioning would have to start in the morning.

"And if the Postmaster won't give me authority to take everyone's fingerprints, I'll get it from the Home Secretary in person," Roger growled.

Carmichael looked almost on the point of tears.

Roger didn't go back to the Yard, but telephoned from River Way. There was a report from Silver: Didi Ames wasn't appearing at the night club after all, because the snow had left the West End deserted. She was back at home, and Silver sounded dispirited.

"All right, I'll go and see her," Roger said. "Might be able to scare her into talking."

He saw the dancer.

Undoubtedly she was a beauty, but he didn't get the same impression as he had out of the photograph. She was as hard as they came, and clever with it.

Yes, Derek Bryant had often been here, she said. He'd thrown his money about, and how was she to know if he hadn't come by it honestly? Yes, his father had called to beg her to let his son go.

"As if I cared," Didi Ames said expressionlessly.

She swore she had no idea where Derek was now. She denied that she'd had a stranger here tonight; he must have gone to the other flat.

That was all; and there wasn't another thing that the police could do.

Roger left, driving through snow already inches thick, and coming down fast. He called at the Fulham Police Station, and checked the day's reports from the men who had watched 72 Clapp Street since the attack on May. There was nothing remarkable, but he saw that young Micky Bryant had been out between half past five and half past nine; and within those hours a youth had called at the St. John's Wood house.

"I'll have a word with Micky Bryant soon," Roger said to the Night Inspector at the station. "What about your chaps watching tonight? Can you get them under cover?"

"Oh, yes, if that's all right with you," the Fulham man said.

"No use to us if they freeze to death," Roger said, and grinned.

But he didn't feel like grinning.

A call to the hospital brought reassuring news

about Kilby; there was a fracture of the skull, but no cause for alarm. Two blows had crashed Tom Bryant's skull; one had cracked Kilby's.

Why had his assailant left him alive?

Had something been hidden in that store room?

A night squad would go over it as with a small-tooth comb and would get Roger out of bed if anything was discovered. Bed? He was tired, but not by any means tired out, and there was still a job to do.

He drove through the heavy snow, finding it easier than he had expected; the snow was soft under the wheels, and wasn't yet icy. There was no traffic about, and he passed the end of Bell Street and headed for Fulham. When he reached Clapp Street, he saw one of the constables sheltering in the doorway of a house opposite.

"They're going to see if they can't get you inside somewhere," Roger said. "Everything all right?"

"As far as I know, sir. That Mrs. Trentham's there—she's a sticker, if ever there was one! Young Micky's been out, and just got back, left his bike in the porch as if he might be going out again, but it's a hell of a night for that."

"It could be because he doesn't want to let the snow melt in the hall," Roger said practically.

"Didn't think of that, sir. So it could. Mrs. Bryant's out; I had a word with her. Miss Harrison's much better, but I expect you know that."

"Yes. Well, I hope they find you somewhere where you can thaw out."

Roger walked round to the back of the house, and had a word with the constable in the service alley. The wind was whipping along here, much worse than at the front.

173

"If they can't think of anything better I should arrange with Mrs. Bryant to stay in the kitchen," Roger said. "You'll be able to do as much there as anywhere else."

"Very thoughtful of you, sir. Not *expecting* more trouble, are you?"

Roger said: "Trying to make sure that it doesn't come, that's all. Good night."

"Good night, sir."

Roger walked back to the street. He could call and have a word with Micky now, but it was very late, and it would disturb the whole household. With a man back and front, what could go wrong? He had a look at Micky's bicycle. An old waterproof sheet was thrown over it, already covered with snow.

He could have arranged for a man to be on duty to follow Micky if the lad went out again, but was there any real justification? The house was the target, wasn't it?

He made his mistake, and decided to do nothing more tonight.

The windshield of his car was thick with snow and he scraped it off with his hands before setting the wipers going.

It was half past eleven when he reached home. Janet was in the front room, with a roaring fire, the newspapers and a magazine. She was flushed and looked as contented as she did snug. She'd had the next-door neighbors in for an hour, the boys had been out in the snow until half past nine, and would probably be difficult to wake in the morning. The only things she had to get now were the crackers; some shops would start selling off at a

174

discount on Christmas Eve, and she was going to wait.

Janet's voice, a whisky and soda and the fire thawed Roger out completely, and made him forget even the cause of the breaking-in at Clapp Street.

He didn't give Micky Bryant another thought.

The constable who had been on duty at the back of 72 Clapp Street was now stationed in the back room of a house on the other side of the service alley, with an electric fire and a gas ring, some cocoa, sandwiches and, secretly, a whisky flask in his hip pocket. The constable at the front of the house had a large room, and brandy instead of whisky. Both of them sat in the gloom, watching the little house and seeing it and the houses nearby showing up pale and ghostly. It was the man at the front who saw a light go on, about half past twelve, and who sat up and peered out. It was snowing more heavily than ever, but he could see clearly, because the street lamps had been left on.

The front door opened.

Micky Bryant came out, and closed the door behind him. He did that very slowly and stealthily, and the watching policeman felt almost certain that he was trying not to make any noise. When the door was closed, the lad stood and looked back, as if expecting to see it open again; or expecting to hear a call.

Nothing happened.

The bicycle had been thrust deeply into the narrow porch. Micky took the waterproof off, and tossed it in a corner, then wheeled the machine out into the snow, which was at least four inches deep.

Micky switched on the front lamp and mounted the machine; but he slipped and fell.

He got up, and pushed the machine toward the gate post, but he couldn't avoid the policeman who came hurrying from his hiding place.

"Bit late out, son, aren't you?" he asked. "No trouble inside, I hope."

"No, not really," Micky said. He stared into the policeman's face, and his expression gave no hint of the fast beating of his heart. "They're all asleep."

"Bed's not a bad place on a night like this, son." The policeman was obviously puzzled. "Where—"

"Listen," Micky said in what seemed a burst of confidence, "don't give me away; Mum—Mum wouldn't understand. I've hardly seen my girl since I've been home; she lives Edgware Road way. I can be back before Mum wakes. Be a pal."

The policeman was an understanding man.

He found himself grinning.

Crafty little so-and-so, young Micky Bryant.

To look at him, you wouldn't think that he had anything in him, but even the snow wasn't going to keep him away from his girl. Quite a girl she must be, too.

"Okay," he said.

"Thanks ever so," Micky said gratefully, and mounted his machine.

Soon the red light disappeared.

The constable went in again.

There was just the rustle of the falling snow and the pale unreal darkness.

The warmth of the little room beckoned him.

It was when he was in the Wandsworth Bridge Road, not far from his home, that Micky noticed that he was being followed; or at least that some-

176

one was cycling after him. He heard nothing; but twice, when the other passed beneath a street lamp, he caught a glimpse of him there. He wasn't worried. He had the key tucked safely in his pocket, and there was the strength of his purpose to make him forget the cold, the snow, the slippery road. He pedaled on, looking round every now and again, and fancying that he caught sight of the other man.

He wasn't quite sure.

It would take him three quarters of an hour to reach the house in St. John's Wood, and he knew that it was no use hurrying. He didn't want to be too tired, either, for there might be a fight.

He had more than the key in his pocket; he had a sheath knife.

The familiar roads had a strange look tonight, and he had never known London so deserted. There wasn't a sound, except that soft rustling. Once, crossing a main road, he saw the lights of a car. When he looked behind him, the road was as empty as the road ahead. False alarm then; the other cyclist had been someone going home late.

He drew near the Edgware Road. Five cars went crawling one after another, and they lit up the road a long way ahead. The scene was lovely, but Micky didn't think about that; just the task of getting to Derek.

He turned off the main road.

In the side streets it was dark.

Then he reached the corner of the street where the woman lived. No lights were on, and until he was close to the gate he couldn't be sure which house it was; but there was a lighted window at a front room.

He plowed on toward the gate, which was wide open. He shone his torch, and made out the number: 18. This was it. The blinds were drawn at the window but he saw them move, suddenly— and he saw Didi standing there and looking out. Then a skid made the bicycle slither. He tried to recover his balance, felt the back wheel skid, then gave up the attempt and prepared to fall. The snow was so deep that there wasn't any chance of hurting himself. He managed to jump clear of the bicycle. The light didn't go out, but snaked along the snow and shone upon a bush which looked as if it was made of cotton wool.

He looked up at the window.

Yes, there she was, standing there and staring, she—

He heard a sound—a thud and a cry, which was cut off short. He swung round. In the gloom he saw a man falling; he didn't know that it was the C.I.D. man who was watching, and who had moved to get a closer view. He saw two other men—the huge George, standing over the man on the ground, and Sammy rushing at him from the wall, where he had been hiding.

16

Fight to Death

Micky saw the dark figure rushing toward him with an arm upraised and a weapon in it. He couldn't tell what the weapon was. The light from the window and the light from the cycle lamp were just enough to show that he had been out in the snow for a long time; his shoulders were covered with it and the front of his coat seemed to hold as much snow as Micky's.

Micky was still on the ground.

He kicked the bicycle free, and lay on his back, and Sammy seemed to think that he was stunned, for he didn't slacken his pace, just came on as if one smashing blow would be enough.

Micky shot out his foot.

Sammy saw it, and dodged to one side. He slipped in the snow. One moment he had been a rushing menacing figure, and the next he was just a lout staggering about, arms waving as he tried to keep his balance. The weapon glinted in the light, and Micky knew that it was metal, guessed that it was an iron bar. He scrambled desperately to his

179

feet, and tore at his coat to get the knife. Before he had it out, Sammy recovered. Iron bar raised, he was only a couple of yards in front of Micky. He was grasping for breath; he wore a scarf over his face, with slits for the eyes and another for the mouth. He wore a knitted balaclava helmet, too, which made him look almost like a hooded creature from another world.

Micky touched the knife.

Sammy leaped, arm swinging.

Micky swayed right, deceived the other, and darted toward the left. He got his knife out, in the same moment. He heard the swish of the iron bar. Snow clogged his shoes. At any other time it would have been easy, but he just couldn't move fast enough. But he had the knife, and turned to face Sammy.

He kicked into a drift, and pitched forward.

One moment there was a fifty-fifty chance; next, he was half buried in soft, powdery snow, and the knife dropped from his fingers. He pictured Sammy smashing at his head with the iron bar, and raised his own arms and folded them over his head. The weapon smashed down on his left arm. The pain made him cry out. Fear gave him new strength. He squirmed round, just able to see the man holding the weapon high, and he flung his arm up.

He caught the other's wrist.

The blow was checked in mid-air, and they made a kind of tableau, with Micky on his back, head and shoulders off the snow, right hand thrust upward like a ramrod, and Sammy struggling desperately to get free.

He kicked savagely.

180

Micky felt the kick in his ribs, but snow on the cap of the other's boot saved him from its full force. The kick made the other overbalance, and Micky had a chance which wasn't likely to come again. He tightened his grip on Sammy's wrist, and twisted. He heard the other squeal, and saw him stagger. Then Sammy collapsed in the snow, falling across Micky's legs. Micky fought to get himself free, fought to draw himself to safety, but couldn't. The other had squirmed round in turn. He had lost his weapon, but his hands were at Micky's throat.

Micky could hear his harsh, squeaky breathing.

Micky was lying on his back, with the other on top of him, and they struggled for what seemed age-long time. The grip at Micky's neck was getting tighter and tighter, and he could feel the constriction at his lungs. He remembered that this had happened to May, that she nearly had been strangled. He kept the muscles of his neck as taut as he could, and tried desperately to breathe but could only draw a wheezy breath. The tightness at his lungs was getting more painful. There were lights in front of his eyes, white and red specks which kept moving about. There was pain at his heart and pain at his neck and pain at his ears and his eyes. His own right hand was just beneath the other man's chin; he was thrusting upward as hard as he could; only that was preventing the other from finishing him off, but—Sammy was trying to kill him. Kill him, then get the key—

Had something like this happened to Derek?

It *had*, to his father.

In the awful struggle, Micky had forgotten George. Recollection brought an onrush of new

181

fear. He couldn't last much longer, even against Sammy, who had managed to get his weight on Micky's arm; his elbow was beginning to bend.

Micky seemed to gather up his whole body, and heave upward, his hand at Sammy's chin and all his weight behind that one effort. He felt a screaming pain at his shoulder, and he also felt despair.

But a miracle happened.

The weight eased, and he pushed harder.

Sammy sagged back. The grip at Micky's throat slackened. The pains faded. Micky pushed again, and the other toppled to one side and then fell sluggishly into the snow. He didn't move. It was almost impossible to believe but it was true; Sammy lay still in the snow, in a peculiar position, and with his head at a strange angle, not straight on his neck.

There were pains and strange noises in Micky's head. He tried to get up, only to drop back again, but it didn't matter.

Where was George? That other, falling, man? The woman?

Micky did not know how long he lay there, gasping for breath. Every moment he expected Sammy to get up and start again; or big George to come.

Micky got up, slowly, feeling sick.

He stood swaying, with his feet wide apart. He couldn't go through that again; he must find his knife. Pity he hadn't a gun. In his weakness, he knew that he would be no match for George; or for anyone. The dream of saving Derek had faded in the sick realization that he'd been a crazy fool.

He must go the police.

Why wasn't George here? Who was the man who had fallen into the snow?

He wasn't there now; George must have taken him away.

Micky looked back at Sammy, who hadn't moved. Funny. His scarf was still in position, but the eyeholes had slipped down, his—his nose was poking through one of them.

Funny!

Then Micky noticed the position of the head and the neck. He realized what had happened, that it wasn't funny at all.

His heart was beating heavily and painfully. Movement was difficult, and he couldn't control his feet in this damned snow.

He forced himself to move more quickly, and felt better. He picked the bicycle up and walked toward the gate, beginning to shiver, as much with reaction as with the cold; his body was warm, but his hands were lumps of ice. He had to lean against one of the gate posts. If only someone would come along. What wouldn't he give for the sight of a copper! Fool, fool, fool!

He did not realize that he was terribly frightened, as he moved away from the gate.

Then a car turned the corner.

At first, he couldn't believe it, but there it was, the sidelights showing clearly against the whiteness; then the headlights were switched on as the car came crunching steadily over the frozen snow. Here was help!

The car was coming slowly, its engine loud. Micky raised a hand, but he felt sure that the man had seen him. Why, the car was turning this way!

The car was turning this way, and coming faster.

Fear exploded into terror.

"*No!*" screamed Micky. "*No!*"

He knew George was in that car.

He turned and ran, but was caught in the beam of headlights and his own shadow was black and hideous against the snow. He slipped, gasped in dread, recovered—and then kicked against Sammy's body.

He couldn't save himself from falling, but he was up in a flash, with that awful light on him. If only he could get to the wall and climb over.

He leaped for the wall, scrambled to the top, and fell backward. He didn't have a chance, now, but at least he had saved himself from being crushed. He saw other shadows. The car had stopped. A large man was rushing from the car. George.

Micky felt a blow on the head, and fell. He was vaguely aware of other lights, far off, and a man's hands at his body, searching—searching for the key, that accursed key.

Roger West woke a little after seven o'clock, and wondered why everything seemed so light, for mornings were dark at this time of the year. Then he realized that light from the street lamps was reflected from the snow; so was the light from a nearby window.

The boys, of course.

He grinned.

Janet stirred, but was still asleep. Roger pushed the bedclothes back and got out of bed, yawned, dragged on his dressing gown, and went out. The boys were talking in undertones, and their door

184

was tightly closed. He didn't let them know that he was coming, but opened the door very stealthily.

They were standing by the open window, wearing only pajamas. Scoopy had his slippers on; Richard was barefooted. Roger heard a giggle, and saw Scoopy draw his hand back. He hurled a snowball out.

"Whose window are you after?" Roger asked.

They both spun round.

There was a moment's startled silence; then Richard smiled and said perkily: "Hallo, Dad, it didn't turn to rain."

"I'll turn you to rain if there's any more of this nonsense," Roger said. "Shut the window, put some clothes on, and try to get some sense into your thick heads—that's the way to catch cold and if you catch one, you'll keep everyone awake at night with your coughing, Scoop. If you're still young enough to want to play with the snow, put on your old coats, old gloves and Wellingtons, and throw the snowballs at each other."

Before he had finished, Scoopy was streaking for the clothes, neatly folded on a chair by the side of his bed.

Richard was jumping up and down, in delight. "Oo, Dad, may we?"

"If your mother had caught you doing that she would probably have made you stay in bed for the rest of the day," Roger said. "Don't make too much noise, she's asleep." He went out, looking at the letter box as he walked down the stairs. He was still yawning. The newspapers weren't poking through; everything was likely to be late in this weather. He went into the kitchen, put on a kettle and, instead of his morning glance through the newspapers to find out how things were in crime, he went to the telephone in the front room, and called the Yard.

The Night Duty Superintendent said brightly: "So you wake up some mornings....Not much in for you yet, but I haven't heard from St. John's Wood yet. Let's see—young Lothario Micky Bryant left his home at 12:34 last night, on his bicycle, said he'd got a girl friend and don't tell his Mum. No report that he's back yet. Like me to ring them and call you back?"

"I'll call them," Roger said, slowly.

He didn't like it at all. Micky Bryant seemed about the last one in the world to spend a night with a girl, as things were at home.

Roger rang the Fulham Station, and while he was holding on, he heard Richard come down the stairs, humming. Then a door slammed. Next, the Fulham Night Duty sergeant said: "Got no report that young Bryant returned, sir, but King—that's the officer who reported him leaving—is still in Clapp Street. Shall I go and send a man to find out what happened?"

"What time's King due to be relieved?"

"Eight o'clock, sir."

"Send a man," decided Roger, "and ring me back quickly, will you?"

He was frowning when he went into the kitchen. He could hear the boys laughing out in the garden —and then he scowled; one of them had turned the kettle out, instead of turning it down. He picked it up, and found it empty.

His eyes lit up.

"Bless 'em," he said, "they've made the tea." He poured out a cup of tea, sipped it slowly; and then heard a banging sound from above his head. Janet was awake. He took the tray upstairs, and saw her lying snug, hair dark and untidy against the pillow. He tossed her a bed jacket and watched her sit up, answered her sleepy questions about the snow, the boys, how he had slept; he drank the tea with lazy enjoyment—and the telephone bell rang. He picked up the instrument by the bedside.

"West speaking."

"Fulham Station, sir, reporting as promised. There's no report that young Bryant got back to the house, neither from King or Sharples—Sharples was at the back. The boy's bicycle isn't in the yard or in the porch where it was last night."

Roger said, very softly: "Damn, oh damn," fell silent for a moment, and then went on: "Right, thanks. I'll go over to Clapp Street."

He rang the hospital, and got a good report on Kilby. Something on the credit side, he thought bitterly. If Micky Bryant was hurt—

What the hell would his mother feel?

Mrs. Bryant had obviously been up for some time when Roger arrived. She was dressed, but hadn't a dust cap or the apron on; she wore a black sweater and skirt and a black-and-white scarf; and the brightness of the morning showed him how clear and blue were her eyes. She was surprised to see him, just as she had been before, but she didn't keep him waiting on the porch.

So she hadn't missed Micky.

One of the children upstairs was shouting, and another giggling. He recognized the tone; they were on the edge of a quarrel, when laughter would turn to tears, and parents either suffered nervous tension or, if they were lucky, hardly noticed the noise.

Mrs. Bryant ushered him into the bravely decorated front room.

"Is it bad news of Derek?" she asked, very quietly.

"No," said Roger, "there's still no word. Do you know where Micky is?"

"Don't be ridiculous," Mrs. Bryant said. "He's upstairs in his bed."

"Are you sure?"

She didn't answer.

He judged from that that she wasn't absolutely sure, that she had taken it for granted that her son was in his room. She turned and hurried out of the room and up the stairs, with Roger following. She had nice legs, neat, young-looking ankles. Roger watched from the door of the stairs, heard her move sharply across the little landing and then the squeak of a door.

Silence.

It lasted for a long time.

Roger started up the stairs. Mrs. Bryant came toward him when he reached the landing, and the old, familiar pallor was back.

"I'd no idea he'd gone out," she said, in a stony voice.

"Have you any idea where he might have gone?"

She said: "No. No, none at all."

Roger said nothing, just watched her. He hated the need for adding to her anxiety, but found himself wondering again whether she had lied to him before this morning; and whether she was lying now. Her eyes glittered so.

"Has he a girl friend?" Roger asked.

"No—no one he would visit at that hour, anyhow."

"Are you sure?"

"Yes," she said. "Why—why did you think—"

He told her of Micky's sortie, and of his pleading with a policeman.

The threatened uproar started in the other room—shrieking and crying, and "*I hate you, I hate you!*" time and time again. It might have been a thousand miles away.

Mrs. Bryant was frightened, and Roger sensed that she was more vulnerable than at any time since he had known her.

"Mrs. Bryant," he said, "this is a most united family, and one I like very much, but inexplicable and ugly things have happened. We've never discovered why your husband was killed. We don't know what Miss Harrison's assailant was after. If we knew the motive for the murder or the breaking and entering, we might be able to prevent more trouble. We've reason to believe that the mystery is connected with the Post Office, and it might be extremely grave. If there is anything at all you can tell us, to keep it back would be failing in your duty to your children as well as to the community."

He stopped.

Had it been too formal? Pompous? Would that approach have been right for Bryant but not for her?

Her eyes burned.

"I can well believe that you and either of the elder children would do anything out of a sense of loyalty to Mr. Bryant," Roger went on, "but—"

189

She cried: "Please don't go on!"

One child was crying and another was soothing; in another world.

"I don't know of any reason why my husband should have been murdered and I don't know any reason why Micky should be out all night, but—I came across something yesterday which *might* be what that thief wanted." Mrs. Bryant turned toward the bedroom door. "I'll show it to you. It was hidden among our—our personal papers and souvenirs. Tom must have put it there. I don't know why and I don't know what key it is."

Roger echoed sharply: "Key?"

"Yes," she said.

The bed had been turned back, and, in spite of the bitter cold, a window had been flung wide open; it was almost as cold in the bedroom as it was out in the street. There were the photographs and the little personal touches inseparable from the home—and the cardboard box. She took it down and rummaged through some papers and oddments.

She stopped.

Soon, she moved the papers aside more carefully and Roger heard her catch her breath.

She didn't need to tell him that the key was gone.

17

Mad Morning

Roger's car crunched over the slush outside the Yard's main steps, and he stopped a foot from the wall. The middle of the yard was almost clear of snow, after salt and gravel had been spread, but the sides were piled high, and there were patches of pure white. The sky was still overcast, threatening more snow. A policeman was busy with a shovel on the steps of the C.I.D. building.

Roger got out, and opened the door for Mrs. Bryant.

She had said very little since she had discovered that the key was missing. The ever-ready Mrs. Trentham had come to the rescue; now, while the children were being given their breakfast, Mrs. Bryant stepped out of the car and looked up at the massive gray building.

"First time you've visited us, isn't it?" Roger asked, and took her arm as they walked over some slush toward the steps. "It's better going here," he went on. "I'll be able to tell you in five minutes whether there's any news of Micky or Derek."

191

She didn't speak.

"What I told you in the car, I meant," Roger said, as they neared the top of the steps. A gust of wind cut over from the river, and he shivered in the teeth of it, and hustled Mrs. Bryant into the overheated hall. "No one is going to blame you for anything. If your husband was involved with criminals, which I think most unlikely, I'll do my best to keep his name free from scandal. We'll all try to help Micky, too, whether he's in a scrape or not. And there's only one reason why I've brought you here: to try to identify the key you saw in that box."

They were walking toward the lift.

"I understand," Mrs. Bryant said in a low voice, "and you're very good."

He took her into one of the waiting rooms, where there was a telephone and a small desk. It was very warm, but she didn't loosen her dark blue coat or her scarf. Roger took his coat off and flung it over a chair, and sat down. He pressed a bell, and a constable came in almost at once.

"Tea for two and some toast," Roger said, "and make it snappy." He nodded as the constable went out, then picked up the receiver. He had never felt more desperate with the need for doing a dozen things at once; the years had taught him to take the crazy days slowly at the start, and get the right perspective.

He called Turnbull.

"Micky Bryant went out in the early hours of this morning and hasn't come back," he said. "He was out last night between half past five and ten-nish, too. Drop everything and try to trace his movements. He was on his bicycle, both times, and the bike's also missing. It was a Midge, pale blue with a red line, drop handlebars, two years old. You've pictures and descriptions of the boy. Get moving."

"I'm on my way," Turnbull said.

Roger rang off, but plucked the receiver up again at once and asked: "Is the Assistant Commissioner in, do you know?...Good, ring through to his secretary and say I'll be along in five minutes." He rang off, stood up and lit a cigarette, then darted toward the telephone again and said: "Give me Mr. Morris." He drew hard at the cigarette, watched all the time by Mrs. Bryant. "Hallo, Morris, West here....How's that collection of keys? Still in glass cases?...Good. I want you to let Mrs. Bryant see it; she'll be up with you in ten minutes or so....Good man, thanks." He rang off again, drew deeply at the cigarette, and said: "Practically every type of key is kept in the collection here, Mrs. Bryant; you might be able to recognize the type from that, and when we can show you Post Office originals, you'll find it easier to identify. Sure there's nothing else you can tell me?"

"Absolutely nothing," Mrs. Bryant said, almost humbly. "Mr. West—" She hesitated.

"Yes?"

"You won't hide anything about Derek or Micky from me, will you?"

"Nothing at all," Roger promised. He glanced at his watch; and then the constable came in with a tea tray and toast under a silver-plated cover: service usually reserved for the hierarchy. "You take your time over this," Roger said to Mrs. Bryant, "and when you've finished, the constable will take you to see the keys. Detective Inspector Morris is

193

expecting Mrs. Bryant," he added to the police-man. "I'll join you there."

"Very good, sir."

Once in the passage, Roger was at Chatworth's door in two minutes, tapped, and opened the door without a summons. Chatworth was with his secretary, a no-nonsense forty in white blouse and black skirt. Obviously she had been given her instructions, for she said: "I'll be back in a moment, sir."

"Right." Chatworth had a sleek, shiny, polished look, and a bow tie, red with white spots, hid coyly behind his double chin. He was dressed in navy blue, and looked quite the high executive. "Well, what's the hurry?" he asked as the door closed.

Roger said: "I won't go into detail, but Mrs. Bryant found a key at the house a day or two ago, and it could be the thing the thief was after. Her second son's disappeared, with the key. I'd like her to be able to examine all the types of keys used by the Post Office; we might get an idea of the trouble to expect, but—" he had hardly paused for breath, but this time gave Chatworth a chance to speak; Chatworth let it pass. "I don't want Carmichael at River Way to know what we're doing. In fact I'd rather it was done at one of the other offices, if the same types of keys are used, and I wouldn't carry enough authority to arrange it."

Chatworth said: "Hum," and then slowly put out a hand toward the telephone. "Well, you wouldn't ask for that if you didn't think it necessary. I'll have a word with the Postmaster General's office."

He lifted the receiver.

"While you're on to the P.M.G.," said Roger, "you

194

might tell him that this morning we're going to take the fingerprints of everyone on the payroll at River Way."

Chatworth was holding on for his call.

"You know what the P.M.G.—"

"I don't care if they're still delivering Christmas parcels on New Year's Day," Roger said. "We've got to have that job done this morning; we were fools to let them stop us before."

Chatworth didn't speak, until his call came through.

Then he was brisk, crisp and decisive.

"...well, please yourself, but we'll take it to Cabinet level if needs be." He listened, and then went on: "Good. See that Farnley gets a note, will you? And the keys...Good." He rang off, and glowered. "Why do you always get what you want instead of a kick in the pants? They'll send a note authorizing the Postmaster at City Central to show you all the types of keys, and they're exactly the same kind as those used at River Way. It's an identical office. And you heard about the other."

Roger jumped up.

"Thanks, sir," he said, and turned to the door. "All right for me to leave?"

He arranged for the lock and key expert at the Yard to take Mrs. Bryant to the City Central Post Office. Then he looked in at his office, to check the post—and found Silver by the desk, saying into the telephone: "I don't care if he's with the Commissioner himself, get him on the line."

Roger let the door close behind him. Silver didn't notice him at first, but he didn't like what he saw of Silver: the glittering eyes, the taut lips, the urbanity all gone. So this was more bad news; and Silver had been in search of Micky Bryant.

Silver saw him, stiffened, and then slowly put the receiver down. As Roger went nearer, the other man said:

"The St. John's Wood man watching Didi's flat was killed last night. Skull smashed. There'd been a fight in the garden of the house. Micky Bryant's cap was found there. So was his bicycle. He's missing. I've seen Didi Ames, and she says she doesn't know a thing. I'd like a warrant to search both flats at that house."

"See Chatworth," Roger said. "He'll play."

In spite of grit and salt, the drive along the Embankment to River Way was a nightmare. It was freezing harder than ever, and car after car turned in a gentle skid and went into the curb at either side. Heavy traffic was pulled up alongside the river, the drivers taking no chances. The Thames looked like watery ice, as if it would freeze over if the cold weather continued. Everyone whom Roger passed was huddled up, chilled, miserable.

A long line of red Post Office vans queued outside the entrance with as many covered lorries all carrying red POST OFFICE printed labels. Drivers and men stood about or stamped up and down, banging their arms across their chests. As he drew nearer, Roger saw why. A big van had skidded into a post, and was blocking traffic both ways. He called a policeman to take his own car to the end of the line, squeezed past the wreckage where seven or eight men were busy, and hurried toward the loading platforms, slipping as he went. He expected to find Carmichael in a rage or at least a

196

flurry. Instead, the little man was superintending the loading of some vans in his calmest mood. He was muffled up in a thick belted topcoat and a bulging brown scarf and he wore a bowler hat. His ears looked as red as a woman's varnished nails, and the shine on his nose would have pleased any brewer. There were twenty or more vans and lorries in the yard, where the loading and unloading were going smoothly.

Roger was outwardly as calm.

"Ah, good morning," Carmichael said, and added with gentle malice: "Didn't think it would be too long before you arrived, Mr. West."

"Morning," Roger said. "Why aren't you tearing your hair?"

"How little you know of the problems that confront us here," said Carmichael. "The danger was that we might get choked, Mr. West, but this morning we shall be practically clear before the next deliveries arrive. Once clear, we can keep the flow going."

"That's good," Roger said, "we needed a clear spell, too." He told Carmichael what he was going to do, and saw the man's eyes narrow as if with utter dismay.

"We want just one man with a certain fingerpoint, that's all," Roger said, "and we've got to find him."

"Very well, if it must be, it must be," Carmichael said thinly.

"Thanks." Roger hesitated, and then said very slowly and deliberately: "How far do you think Miss Deirdre Ames can be trusted, Mr. Carmichael?"

Carmichael stood very still. His gaze didn't falter. His hands did not move.

"I think the best thing is to set up your equipment in the canteen," he said, carefully. "It is the most convenient place, and the process won't get in the way of the mail. However, I'm not very sanguine of results if you want a complete coverage, Mr. West. At least six of the temporaries have telephoned to say that they can't get in this morning, two regulars are down with influenza, and several men haven't turned up or taken the trouble to send a message. It's always like this with a fluctuating staff. I am sure that Mr. Farnley would agree that we must do everything we can to co-operate, and I will readily volunteer to have my prints taken first."

There was no way to force him or Didi Ames to talk; yet.

Three Yard men arrived, and Roger had the fingerprinting started before he left; Carmichael's first. There were a few grumbles, but no one positively refused to have his prints taken. When Roger left, a little after half past ten, snow had started to fall again, and the sky was so dark that it was hard to realize it was mid-morning. There was no sense in trying to hurry. He took half an hour to reach the Yard, left the car in a convenient place for driving off again, and went straight up to the engineers' department, and the keys.

Mrs. Bryant was waiting.

She had selected a key which was very much like the one she had seen in the box.

An hour later, at the City Central Office, she picked out a similar key. A gray-haired, brown-eyed Post Office official, who had a runny cold, put it aside and said nothing while Mrs. Bryant was there, but his glance at Roger suggested that he had plenty to say.

He took Roger into another office.

"Chief Inspector," he said solemnly, "this key is the master key to all London Post Office vans. A driver who has locked his rear doors might reasonably feel secure in leaving the car, but with this key, any van could be unlocked and registered packages taken out in a matter of minutes. Almost, in seconds! There is one such key in each main post office, in the custody of the Chief Sorter. Had one been reported missing I am quite sure that I would have heard, but if you care to telephone the Postmaster General's office, you could make sure of that."

"Thanks," said Roger. "I will."

He telephoned at once, and was told that no theft had been reported. But Mrs. Bryant was quite sure that it was the same kind of key, and there was none other like it in the Post Office selection.

"If the killers have had it for ten minutes they'll have had an impression made, and with a master and a couple of good locksmiths they can turn keys out by the dozen," Roger told Chatworth, and went on: "We should make the strongest recommendation that all locks be changed as soon as possible, sir."

Chatworth said sharply: "It'll take days!"

"Until it's done every G.P.O. van needs a special

guard, and that will take some organizing, too. Sorry, sir, but—"

"I'll do what I can," Chatworth said, "but don't overlook the fact that some people will expect us to find the missing key, and stop any duplicates being made." He wasn't simply being sarcastic.

"Couldn't agree more, sir," Roger said. "I'm going to recommend that we put a general call out to all stations and substations. We want all locksmiths visited, and all known keycutters, and we want to find out if anyone has been asked to cut one or more keys which measure up to the following dimensions. It's a Landon make, quadruple notched. . . . " He went into the technicalities. "As soon as we've a photograph I'll send it round, but that information should be enough to go on with."

"I'll see to it," Chatworth said.

"Thank you, sir. Good-b—"

"Hold on!" Chatworth shouted, and Roger just heard him. "You still there? . . . All right, now listen. We've just had a message from St. John's Wood. The body of a youth who might be Micky Bryant has been taken out of the Regent's Canal. We can't be sure, because the face is unrecognizable."

"Mutilated?"

"Crushed. Car wheel, probably. But we must know if it's Micky Bryant. Too small for his brother."

"All right," Roger said. "I'll try to get identification soon. That all, sir?"

"Yes."

"I'll ring you when I've news," Roger said.

He thanked the Post Office official, and then went out, to join Mrs. Bryant.

200

Although he moved quickly, his feet seemed to drag, for this was a job he had no heart for at all. It had to be done: he seemed destined to be the one to take bad news to Kath Bryant. Her eyes were full of shadows and of fear, and the unspoken question in them couldn't have been more stark.

Roger said: "Mrs. Bryant, I'm afraid we're a long way from certain, but we have to check on a body found this morning. The only way to check is to make sure whether Micky had any other identification marks. Had he?"

She stood absolutely still.

Then she said. "Take me with you, please. I will see for myself."

Roger did not argue.

The journey from the City to St. John's Wood was fairly good, for the road had been cleared and there was much less traffic than in normal weather. Snow was still falling lightly.

They reached the police station, and went into the morgue adjoining, where a youth's naked body lay beneath a sheet. The face had been lightly bandaged, and obviously Mrs. Bryant guessed why; but she searched for a spot on the lower abdomen.

Then, she swung round on Roger, her fine eyes blazing.

"It isn't Micky," she cried, "it isn't Micky! And Derek's fair!"

18

The Robberies

Roger drove back to the Yard, sent Mrs. Bryant home with a driver, then hurried along to his office and was greeted by three men all speaking at once. He sensed the change in their manner; sensed crisis. This was a different element, and yet it didn't surprise him. For days the tension had been increasing remorselessly.

At first it was just something in the manner of the trio, a kind of suppressed excitement.

"Chatty wants you."

"You heard, Handsome?"

"Now she blows."

Roger looked at the C.I. who had said, "You heard, Handsome?" and asked: "Heard what?" His heart was thumping.

"Five P.O. vans robbed," one said, explosively.

"Five different parts of London," another chimed in. "What a hell of a day for it!"

Now it càme like a blast of hot, gritty air. *Five Post Office vans robbed*. If they had said fifty, the effect could hardly have been harsher.

Roger said: "A hell of a day's right," and turned away, almost running along the corridor. He had to pass the lift to get to Chatworth's office, and as it drew up to the floor level Silver appeared. There was snow on his Homburg and his beautifully cut coat but he was still immaculate.

"Handsome!"

Roger turned his head. "Can't wait—" he began, then saw who it was, and waited. "P.O. vans are being raided all over London., You got anything new?"

"Could be. A car was seen driving away from Didi Ames's place last night. Neighbor who couldn't sleep saw a man being forced into it. Nervous type, didn't say a word until we questioned people with windows overlooking the house."

"Car identified?" asked Roger.

"An Austin A.40. Carmichael has one. Time we picked him up, isn't it?"

"Yes. And the Ames woman, for questioning. Lay it on."

"Right," said Silver.

"Thanks." Roger went at the double toward Chatworth's office. There was Chatworth with the unfamiliar sleekness, standing at the window this time, and looking round toward the door. As Roger closed it, the telephone bell rang. Chatworth moved slowly, and picked up the receiver.

"Assistant Commissioner," he announced, and his manner bordered the ponderous.

He listened.

"All right," he said, "do what you can." He put the receiver down, and said to Roger in the same tone of voice: "That's the sixth P.O. van raid this morning. This time the driver was injured. Three sacks of registered packets gone. New district this time—Putney. No way of telling how many there'll be, is there?"

"No," Roger said.

"Anything at all to work on?" Chatworth asked. "More than I already know, I mean?"

"Silver is going to pick up Didi Ames at her place, and have a look round. I'm going over to pick Carmichael up for questioning. By the letter of the law we can't raid his flat, but—"

"I'll get a search warrant," Chatworth said. "Is he still at River Way?"

"Yes."

"Bring him here," Chatworth ordered.

The telephone bell rang again.

Roger knew exactly what Chatworth feared, and felt as much on edge. Chatworth took off the receiver.

"Yes," said Chatworth.

"Yes."

"All right, thanks." He rang off, and kept a stubby forefinger on the shiny telephone. "Number 7. Hampstead. No one hurt. For all we know there might be a dozen other robberies taking place at this very minute. Go and get Carmichael. *Don't stand there gawping at me, man, go and get Carmichael!*"

Carmichael was in his office, studying some foolscap sheets of figures when a man came hurrying across the Sorting Office, and his shadow darkened the doorway for a moment. He strode in, and Carmichael looked up—into the rugged face of the van driver Simm. Simm's eyes were glittering, his fingers poked out of khaki mittens and his nose looked like one long dewdrop.

Carmichael was sharp.

"What is it, Simm? I've just five minutes to look at these."

"You haven't got time to look at any documents," roared Simm. "You've got a load of worry. Syd Day's van was robbed, and Syd's got a crack on the head that nearly split it in two. Swine had a master key, got away with—"

He stopped.

Carmichael stood up very quickly; then he pushed past Simm, and stepped toward the door. He tied his muffler more tightly about his neck. Several people in the big Sorting Office, working at a lower tempo than at any time during the past week, looked at him.

He reached the loading platform, but instead of going toward the three vans which had just come in, he turned right toward Goose Lane. He put his bowler firmly on his head, and walked briskly along.

A Yard man wearing an earpiece cap and blue lumber jacket followed Carmichael out of the Post Office yard and into the narrow space of Goose Lane. No one had walked along here for some time. Some sets of footprints showed, covered with the morning's fresh snow. Against one side the snow was a foot deeper than it was against the other wall, and the little alcoves where a man had lurked, before jumping out to kill Tom Bryant, were so packed with snow that they now offered an even better hiding place.

Carmichael tried to walk quickly, but it was

heavy going. Great clumps of snow gathered on his boots, and the ends of his trousers as well as the end of his long topcoat were rimmed with snow. The policeman hung behind. Near the Embankment end of the alley he stepped into one of the alcoves, and Carmichael looked round.

He didn't see the Yard man.

This man followed until Carmichael was walking along the Embankment. He turned off, quite soon, and headed for Sloane Square, then crossed to the Underground Station. The Yard man got on the same train in the next carriage. Carmichael changed at Charing Cross and took a tube for St. John's Wood. As they came out of the station, the Yard man had no time to nip into a telephone box, but he saw a policeman standing at a corner and surveying the desolate scene. He beckoned, and hurried.

"Telephone the Yard, tell Chief Inspector West that Sergeant Brown is following Carmichael, looks as if he's heading for the St. John's Wood house."

The constable, who could make it hard or make it easy, looked flustered for a moment. Carmichael was turning a corner.

Then: "Got it, sir," the policeman said. "You're following Carmichael to the St. John's Wood house."

"Fine, thanks!" Brown turned and hurried—and slipped on a little mound of packed snow which had been missed by a workman's shovel. He didn't fall. When he reached the corner Carmichael was at the far end of this short, wide road. Brown knew where Didi Ames lived; turn right, walk a hundred yards, turn left. He didn't know of any short cut.

He wasn't likely to be recognized, even if Carmichael turned round, but there were so few people about and the streets and the houses here were so white that he felt conspicuous. He turned the next corner. Carmichael was plowing steadily on, but Brown had gained thirty yards or more. One more corner, and the house where the blonde lived would be in sight.

Brown turned it, and saw a red P.O. van just ahead.

A man, standing close to the wall, smashed a blow at Brown's head, and struck him squarely; struck again, and made him crumple up. Brown didn't even see Carmichael. He was almost unconscious when he was lifted by two men and bundled into the back of the van. The door was slammed, one of the men jumped to the wheel and started off.

Roger looked at the policeman who had been on duty at the gates of the River Way Post Office as if he couldn't believe him. The man repeated what he had said, a little hesitantly, but with greater emphasis.

"I'm sure, sir—Mr. Carmichael talked to Driver Simm, and then went toward Goose Lane. Mr. Brown followed him. Simm drove off in a hurry. Half an hour ago, I should think, but it may have been a bit longer. As Mr. Brown was on the job I didn't think I need take a note of the time."

"Quite right." Roger nodded and went across the yard; it had been sanded again and there was little risk of slipping. Vans were chockablock, and so were the parcels on the loading platforms near the chutes. It looked wrong without Carmichael there to direct operations, but the work was being done. Men were shouting more than usual, and as Roger reached the doorway, he heard someone say:

"Six hold-ups, isn't it?"

"Five or six?"

"Can't say I fancy picking up registers today."

"You pick 'em up and like it!"

Roger crossed the sorting office to the staircase and ran up to the canteen, which was on the first floor. The Fingerprints men were standing or sitting about, with little left to do. One man had a long list in front of him, filling three sheets of foolscap.

"Got 'em all?"

"All except three, temporaries still out on delivery," said the man in charge.

"See that print?"

"No." The man was quietly certain.

Roger didn't speak.

There were robberies going on all over London, and somewhere there was bound to be a clearing point. St. John's Wood? Carmichael's place at Paddington? Or somewhere unsuspected? The first two he could cover, but—

The telephone bell rang, and a clerk answered, then held the instrument out toward Roger.

"Scotland Yard for you, sir."

"Thanks." This might be word relayed through Turnbull, Chatworth, anyone.

"West speaking."

"Hi, Handsome!" a man boomed. It was Turnbull. "Picked up a bit of news for you. Description of a pal of Wilson's—could be the one who killed him. P.O. van driver, name of George, outsize, hard voice, short dark hair, blunt features."

"Simm," said Roger, very slowly. "Thanks. Be seeing you."

He put a general call out for Simm, whose van registration number was 20J41, and then went down to the washrooms near the maintenance department, with an official who had a master key. In Simm's locker was a case of tools, knives and a saw. And there was a pair of tight-fitting leather gloves. The fingers of these were intact, but the right thumb and forefinger were peculiar. At first, it looked as if the leather had been worn away, but that wasn't so. Something had been sewn onto the surface. It looked like dried skin, with the ridges of a fingerprint.

It was skin, or something very much like it, and there was a scar in the middle of the thumb. Studying it in the few precious minutes he had to spare, Roger found himself comparing the skin with that of the famous specimen Wilberforce had in Fingerprints; preserved human skin, giving genuine fingerprints.

Was that it?

Chatworth said: "All right, we can check that later. Listen. Brown followed Carmichael; it looks like the St. John's Wood place. Silver's over there already. You go to Carmichael's home first, then to St. John's Wood. And be quick about it. Twenty-one vans robbed so far, only three raiders caught. Thousands of registered letters and parcels, two consignments of diamonds from Hatton Garden, a sack of treasury notes. We mustn't let them get away with this."

"We won't," Roger said.

"We mustn't," Chatworth said. "They'll rub our noses in mud."

"I still hope to find the Bryant boys alive," Roger said acidly. "I'll report when there's news, sir."

19

Carmichael's Home

Roger could ignore Chatworth's order and go straight to St. John's Wood; he wanted to, desperately. But if he missed anything at Carmichael's little house in Paddington, he would be for the high jump. He went out of the office, and saw Turnbull with two Fingerprints men.

"Where to?"

"Paddington," Roger said, "and we're in a hurry. You take one man, I'll take another. I'll follow you, as you've been there."

"Right."

A detective officer whom Roger didn't know well slid in beside him, and was so silent at first that he was obviously feeling awkward. Driving wasn't easy. The D.O. broke the silence in a voice that was a shade too loud.

"Bad show, isn't it, sir?"

"Foul."

"Think we've got any chance of finding out where they're taking the stuff?"

"You can have my head if there isn't," Roger

said, and then something in the man's exclamation made him chuckle. "We'll live it down, in time. Depends what preparations they've made. If you were picking up sacks of registered mail from all over London and wanted to hide them, where would you put them?"

There was a pause. Turnbull's car skidded slightly and Roger slowed down. They were in Belgrave Square, and there were few people about. Outside two of the office buildings were Royal Mail vans, one a small and red-painted one with *ER* and the Christmas post-early posters, the other a big lorry with two youths sitting on a heap of parcels at the back.

The sergeant exclaimed: "In a Post Office van or one of these lorries!"

"Steal a van or paint one to look genuine, or get a lorry and plaster it with those labels, and what could be simpler?" asked Roger. "No one would suspect a Post Office van today, would they?" He flicked the radio on and talked to the Yard. "Suggest to the Assistant Commissioner that all P.O. vans and lorries are halted and searched," he said, then flicked off and turned into Grosvenor Place. They made good speed through the Park and along the Edgware Road.

Turnbull gave him ample notice of the left turn. Soon they were in Paddington, driving along streets of little houses made picturesque by the snow. Turnbull waved Roger down, and they drew up in the middle of one of the narrow streets.

Roger got out.

Turnbull pointed toward a dark little door, then drove on. Roger gave him three minutes to reach the back of the house, and got out of the car. Two women at windows on the other side of the street watched. He knocked and waited; knocked again.

A Post Office van turned into the street.

Roger said: "Watch that van, will you?" He was peering at the number, which was partly obscured by slush and snow. Then he shouted: "Look out, it's Simm's!"

There was the number, unmistakably: 20J41. And there was the big, round-faced driver at the wheel. The killer, the man with the phony finger-prints. He had slowed down, but suddenly put on speed. The harsh note of the engine seemed to shout his fears. Roger made a dash for his own car, and the detective shouted:

"Stop, there! Stop!"

He threw himself forward, as if he were going to try to stop Simm's van with his body. Roger had time to roar: "Come back!'' and paused by his car, almost paralyzed; for the detective slipped as the van came swinging toward him. The detective scrambled toward the pavement, then flopped down. The van flashed past, spattering slush as far as the walls of the little houses. Roger wrenched open the car door and stabbed at the self-starter. Before the Post Office van reached the corner he was on the move. He saw the detective still on the ground, and thought he saw a woman coming out of one of the front doorways. He put his foot down. The van swung round the corner, slithering. Roger felt the front wheels skid, but they steadied. He went round the corner ten yards behind, and saw the van slithering toward one side of the road as an electric milk float came slowly toward it, hugging the crown of the road. The float driver looked terrified.

The van scraped past the milk float, but struck the curb. It began to heel over, and the noise was frightening. The sight of the van, first on its side, toppling, then upside down with its wheels in the air and still going round, seemed to speak of death. Roger stopped his car, which drew across the road, broadside on. He jumped out, and reached the van as Simm, dazedly, freed himself from the driver's cabin.

Though dazed, Simm raised that powerful arm —and the jimmy.

Roger stopped two yards away, stooped down and grabbed some big lumps of frozen snow. He hurled them at Simm. The first flew over the driver's head, the second struck him in the mouth, the third his right eye. Then Roger flung himself at Simm, and knocked the jimmy out of his grasp. They went down, rolling over, kicking and struggling, Roger on top, clawing the man's hands from his throat. Then the Fingerprints man, Turnbull and the milkman came up.

Carmichael was inside the van; unconscious. So was Sergeant Brown.

There were no sacks of registered mail.

Turnbull went to telephone the Yard.

Roger tried four of the keys on Carmichael's ring before he found one that turned the lock of the front door. He stepped inside. It was small and dark. He switched on the lights as he went from room to room. In one of the three small bedrooms he found pictures of Didi Ames looking her loveliest, and all signed *With Love, Didi*. Then he opened the next bedroom.

Micky Bryant lay there on a single bed.

The boy was quite still, and his eyes were closed. He didn't open them, and he looked as pale as death. There was a turban of bandage on his head, an ugly cut in his cheek, and his right arm was bandaged up to the elbow.

He didn't move or flicker his eyelids when Roger spoke to him swiftly, urgently.

The Fingerprints man was just behind him.

"Get a doctor, locally if you can. If you can't get one in a hurry, telephone the Yard. Snap into it." Roger didn't wait to see the man disappear, but looked down at Micky and felt for the lad's pulse.

It was just beating.

By the time a doctor arrived, with Turnbull on his heels, Roger had made sure that there was no stolen mail at the little house. He had confirmed from a neighbor that Carmichael lived alone here. Carmichael had come home during the early hours; the neighbor had heard his car, the Austin A.40, which he garaged nearby.

The doctor took one look at Micky, and said: "We'll get him to St. Mary's; it's the nearest hospital."

Roger said: "Stay with him, and if he breathes a word, make sure you get it down." He left Turnbull and the doctor to arrange for the ambulance, hurried downstairs and into his car. The Fingerprints man and a uniformed policeman were keeping a growing crowd back.

Roger called the detective.

"You didn't get hurt, then?"

"A bruise or two, sir, but I'm all right now."

"When are you going to learn that it's suicide to

215

run at a moving car?" asked Roger, but he grinned. "Good try, and we're getting somewhere." He got in, flicked on the radio, and called the Yard again. There was no response for several seconds, and when it came it was hurriedly:

"Information Room."

"West here."

"Forty-three robberies to date," the radio operator volunteered gustily. "It's driving us crazy. Caught five thieves in all, opening up the vans with master keys, but they haven't told us much. Say they were supposed to wait with the bags which would be picked up by a lorry or a P.O. van."

"Anything from St. John's Wood?"

"No, sir."

"Any of the stolen bags turned up?"

"No, sir." The radio man seemed to fade out, but he was back again in a moment. "The Assistant Commissioner would like a word with you, sir. Will you hold on?"

Roger said: "Yes." He held on for what seemed too long a time, and they were soon heading toward St. John's Wood, going fast. They passed four Post Office vans; the red vans seemed everywhere. So did temporary postmen with armbands.

Chatworth came on. "You there, West?"

"Yes, sir."

"I'm told you've got Carmichael and Simm, the man of the fingerprint."

"Both on a charge, sir."

"Been able to make them talk?"

"Carmichael's unconscious—drugged, I think— and Simm doesn't seem like a talker," Roger said. "I'm on my way to St. John's Wood."

"Don't let me stop you," growled Chatworth.

"And listen: among the goods stolen are the diamonds I told you about, as well as consignments of jewels from five West End jewelers to provincial customers, two hundred and fifty gold watches, two bags of used treasury notes and the Lord knows how much more. I've only got reports on the contents of eleven of the robbed vans." He was talking so quickly that he almost choked. "If we don't get this stuff back soon, we probably won't get it at all."

"Well, we've got Micky Bryant, alive," said Roger edgily. "We can chalk that up on the credit side. Will you have someone get the report from St. Mary's Hospital, and then tell Mrs. Bryant? Thank you." He switched off, lit a cigarette, and glared at the road in front of him, with the snow caked and icy in the middle and banked up on either side.

Then they turned a corner.

A big covered lorry, plastered with *Royal Mail* stickers, was roaring toward them; behind it were two police cars. Beyond that, near Didi Ames's house, men were struggling in the street, and fighting in the garden. The front door of the house stood open, but although Roger saw all this, he did not notice it.

The lorry was only yards away.

Didi Ames was sitting by the driver, mouth wide open, eyes rounded with sharp fear.

If Roger evaded the lorry, the thieves might get away with some of the stuff; if he collided, he would stop the getaway but might not live to learn about his success.

20

The Love of Carmichael

Roger could move which way he liked; into or out of trouble. He needed only a split second for decision. He swung the wheel so that he sent his own car right across the front of the lorry. The detective sat rigid. The front wheels skidded, with a strange gentleness, and Roger put on the brakes. He held his breath until the impact came. The front wheel of the lorry struck the wing of his car and swung it round and round like a spinning top, but it didn't turn over. Out of control, the lorry slithered across the road, crashed into a lamp post, then fell on its side; the wall of a house held it up. The sound of smashing glass, rending metal, shouting people and the whining engines made bedlam.

Roger felt the car steady.

He was still at the wheel, and the detective hadn't moved. He gulped, strained his shoulder back, and then looked at the man.

"Awake?" he asked.

"And you told *me* not to attempt suicide."

Roger grinned.

He opened the door and stepped out, but almost fell, because he was dizzy and his knees weren't as strong as he had expected. He leaped against the open door, watching men from the police cars helping the dazed Didi and the driver of the lorry. Other police were heading for the back of the lorry, and Roger made himself go forward and, taking each step with great care, reached a spot from where he could see inside the truck. A Divisional C.I.D. man had climbed over the tailboard, and was lifting up a green sack; registered mail was nearly always kept in green sacks. He held up another and another, and then turned and yelled:

"There are hundreds of 'em. We must have 'em all!"

"Yes," said Sir Guy Chatworth, "we seem to have them all, Roger. Two hundred and fifty-seven sacks, and the known value of the contents of forty-nine of them comes to over four hundred thousand pounds. The mind of the man who conceived this is something out of the ordinary. Was Carmichael the man behind it, do you think? I can't believe that the postman Simm was."

"I think Simm and the woman were the leaders," Roger said mildly. He sat in Chatworth's office, with a cigarette in his hand and a glass with whisky and soda in front of him. He felt much better, although not really himself. Outside, the snow had stopped, it was nearly dark, and against the light shining out of the window he could see little streams of water; the thaw had set in, and if it continued there would be no need to worry about Her Majesty's mails tomorrow. "I don't know Carmichael's part for certain; he's still unconscious."

"Did he drug himself? Or fall out with the others at the last minute?"

"He may have fallen out with the others, but not at the last minute," Roger said. "Directly I knew that Bryant was killed for the master key, Carmichael was out of the running as a conspirator. He could have passed that key over, or made an impression on soap or wax any time he liked; he was the last man to need to search, let alone kill for it."

Chatworth sat very still.

"We'll have to wait until we get his story," he said at last. "What else has come in?"

"Plenty. The raiders were all set to go days ago but hadn't the key. We've picked up four locksmiths who've been standing by to make keys as soon as they were given an impression. The raiders we've caught all tell the same story—they're members of two East End gangs, primed for this one job. They were standing by, too, and had orders to collect the keys from a central depot this morning. Simm was crafty, and had another meeting place, in Mile End. Each man was given a key, told to raid a van at a certain spot—always at Post Offices known to handle regular consignments of valuables—and to take the swag to St. John's Wood. Each carried a G.P.O. armband for the occasion, and a big sack—to dump the green registered sacks in."

"You've got to hand them one thing," Chatworth said heavily. "Brilliantly organized."

Roger said:"Brilliant's the word."

"Don't yet know what caused Tom Bryant's death, I suppose?"

"No," said Roger, "but one thing has turned up."

"What?"

"Derek Bryant's hands—in the Thames," Roger said heavily. "No doubts about the prints."

Chatworth was quiet for a long time; and then he broke the silence gruffly: "This scar print that Simm used—I've had a talk with Wilberforce. It shook him badly; he's never come across it before except when trying to identify bodies that have been in the water a long time. Macabre business. Simm knew what we all know: the skin off the hands and feet of a body that's been in water for a long time can sometimes be removed intact. Simm removed the skin of a dead man's hand, and found how it could be preserved and toughened. And he saw the advantages of making us look for a man who didn't exist."

"I can guess what a kick he got out of that," Roger said. "I always had the impression that he enjoyed making fools of us."

"Your turn to talk about the last laugh," Chatworth said, with a sniff. "Well, put all the pieces together as soon as you can. Do you seriously doubt whether Carmichael was involved?"

"He's involved with Didi Ames all right," Roger said. "But not with the robberies, or I'll resign and buy that chicken farm."

It took him a day to prove that he was right about Carmichael.

221

"George Simm is one of three brothers," Roger wrote in his report, "and the only one who kept out of jail for so long. His family record is one of persistent antagonism to the police, and his recent statements make it clear that all his life he has planned to make one big haul and then sit back and mock the police. This attitude was reflected in at least three of his actions—the fingerprint of a dead man which he used deliberately and left behind to mystify us, the theft of registered mail from his own van, with a false print to mislead us, and the posting of the parts of Derek Bryant's body.

"The motive of the plot was simple.

"It began when Simm and Deirdre Ames first got to know each other, twelve months ago. Simm used his knowledge of the Post Office procedure to make his plans. His first need was for a master key, and the raids were to take place during the Christmas mail rush, as success depended on the public's familiarity with temporary postmen.

"Simm's original plan was to get the key from Carmichael, who guarded it with extreme care. Deirdre Ames's part was to make Carmichael lose his head and persuade him to let her have the key. That failed. But Carmichael, deeply in love with the woman, did everything he could to keep her. He even spent his life's savings on her, although he knew why she had first encouraged him. The one thing he would not do was to betray his position. His first loyalty was to the Post Office.

"In fact, he was more careful than ever with the key when he realized what Deirdre Ames wanted. He had seen Simm in the St. John's Wood house, and guessed that Simm and Deirdre Ames were in collusion.

"Simm saw that Carmichael could ruin his plans; but realized that Carmichael was on guard against him. So Simm tried a new tack, by using Derek Bryant.

"Derek Bryant was often in Carmichael's office, getting instructions from the Chief Sorter about suboffice maintenance work. He was in a position to take an impression of the master key. Deirdre's beauty went to his head. At her request, he took the impression and made a key—as a mechanic, that was easy for him. Before handing it over, however, he discovered that Deirdre Ames and Simm were living together.

"He rebelled.

"Meanwhile, his father had discovered the association between Derek and Deirdre Ames. He tried to break it, but the woman was indifferent. By this time, Derek Bryant was desperate. He had got deeply into debt, so as to spend money on Deirdre, and his job was in jeopardy. In his desperation, he confessed to his father that, using the master key, he had stolen a registered packet which had contained a hundred pounds in one-pound notes.

"His father made him hand over the money and the key, promising to try to replace the money, and to protect Derek. This was the day before Tom Bryant's murder. Tom took the key and the money home, hid the key, and kept the money while trying to think up a way of paying it back—perhaps

223

even considering accepting responsibility for the theft.

("These details of Bryant's part are largely conjecture," Roger wrote, "arising out of statements made by Deirdre Ames, who has been fully co-operative since her arrest, doubtless to try to save herself from a charge of accessory to murder.")

"Simm heard Bryant and his son talking about what they were planning, and realized that his chances were now very poor. A man of Tom Bryant's caliber might decide to tell the authorities everything, even at the cost of his own or his son's reputation. So Simm killed Tom Bryant. When Derek heard of his father's death, he realized what had happened and rushed to Simm, to try to avenge his father. They met in the stationery store at River Way. Simm overpowered Derek, murdered him, and dismembered the body. He was now practically certain that the key was at Bryant's Clapp Street house, so he sent an associate, a youth named Samuel Webber, to search the house. When Webber failed, Simm decided, in a last throw, to work on Micky Bryant. The results we now know.

"Carmichael, aware that Simm was responsible for the murders but still desperately in love with Deirdre Ames, tried to keep aloof. He had committed no crime and he did not want to betray the woman. He discovered, through a vainglorious boast of Simm's, that Micky was to be used. In the early hours of the morning he went to plead with the woman. His arrival was not reported, as the officer watching the house in St. John's Wood had been savagely attacked earlier in the evening, and his body was later found in the Regent's Park

Canal. So was that of Simm's accomplice, Samuel Webber, but Carmichael was in time to save Micky Bryant. Carmichael still tried to persuade Deirdre Ames not to continue with her plans. Even when the raids began, he went to give her a last chance. His signed statement, supported by one of Simm's other associates, says that if she betrayed Simm and gave up the haul, he—Carmichael—would not call the police.

"Simm had expected such an ultimatum. He lay in wait for Carmichael and the C.I.D. sergeant who was trailing him and, with them both drugged and in the back of the van, went to Carmichael's house. He intended to murder Micky Bryant, who could identify Deirdre and become a vital witness. Simm had earlier killed another associate, Wilson, who had tried to blackmail him.

"In my opinion," Roger's report finished, "we should not prefer a charge against Carmichael but should establish him as a police witness, and so greatly simplify the case for the prosecution."

Roger had several copies of the report made—for Turnbull, for Chatworth, and for Kilby, who was out of the hospital after seven days. The angle of the blow, the thickness of his skull and the fact that Simm had been in a great hurry had saved his life. Simm had attacked him in the stationery store because he had kept some safe-breaking tools behind the racks, which might have had his own prints on them.

Mrs. Bryant took the news as Roger would have expected. At least she had Micky and the younger children, and the devotion of May Harrison, who was to go and live at Clapp Street. Kilby told

Roger that. Kilby seemed likely to spend a lot of time seeing that May didn't grieve too much. There was always the good and the bad.

Two days before Christmas Roger dropped Kilby at the end of Clapp Street, and then drove back to his own home. It was a little after nine o'clock, and the boys might still be up. He hoped they were, for he wanted to see them. They were in the kitchen, Richard with a cartoon page in front of him, Scoopy standing at the table and looking at his mother as she peered into the oven. The smell of cooking was rich and appetizing.

"Oh, hallo, Dad," Scoopy said. "Isn't Mum mean—she won't let me have one of those mince pies."

"I don't want a mince pie," Richard said. "They're too hot."

"You don't mean to say you're home for the day," said Janet, her face flushed and her eyes gay as she straightened up from the oven. "It's only half past nine!"

"I'm home for the night, tomorrow, Christmas Eve and the next day," Roger told her. "All I have to do is turn in my final reports, and I can do that from here tomorrow."

Janet's eyes glowed.

"Oh, that's wonderful! You can help with the last-minute shopping, and—"

"There's one condition," Roger interrupted. "I might find myself recalled to the Yard on urgent business unless you meet it." He winked at the boys.

"I knew there'd be an excuse," said Janet, resignedly. "But let me hear it."

"Two mince pies for me and one each for the boys, right here and now," said Roger.

Scoopy pounced on the pies, while Richard explored carefully for a cool one.

Afterward, when the boys were in bed, Janet took Roger into the front room, where half a dozen parcels from relatives and friends were waiting for the boys to open on Christmas morning. He looked at them speculatively as he sipped his drink.

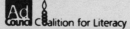